The *New* Unwritten Law

Byron Grush

Published in the United States by Broadhorn Publishing, Delavan, WI

ISBN-10:0-692-80334-3
ISBN-13: 978-0-692-80334-9

Author's Preface

The New York Sun ran an article in September of 1912 in which it quoted Prosecuting Attorney for Cook County (Chicago, Illinois), John E. W. Wayman's comments on the near impossibility of convicting a woman of murder. "Women Jurors Needed To Try Women For Murder," the headline said. Of course, only registered voters could serve as jurors, and women did not yet have the right to vote in these United States. "Men too chivalrous to convict even in cases of guilt," Wayman said. "Thirty-eight women accused of murder acquitted in Chicago in the last nine years and only seven found guilty." And in another article: "The only way to stop husband slaying is to make radical changes in the jury system."

Two years later the situation hadn't improved. Illinois State's Attorney for Cook County, Maclay Hoyne, stated, "The manner in which women who have committed murder in this county have escaped punishment has become a scandal. The blame in the first instance must fall upon the jurors who seem willing to bring in a verdict of acquittal whenever a woman charged with murder is fairly good looking and is able to turn on the flood gates of her tears, or exhibit a capacity for fainting." Some bizarre twist of reverse chauvinism? Or propaganda? Certainly it must have been frustrating for prosecutors whose conviction rate dwindled under the circumstances.

People like Wayman and Hoyne were capable and dedicated public servants, defenders of the law. But often they came up against Chicago's super-lawyers: men like Clarence Darrow and Edgar Lee Masters, whose names and exploits we remember, while the diligence of these notably honest public officials has fallen into obscurity. Which is not to say that there wasn't corruption, negligence and incompetence in the judicial system. There was. Hoyne was lauded for his aggressive investigations into criminal acts within the police department and the courts systems of Chicago and the subsequent successful prosecution of many of the offenders.

Around 1910, a ground-breaking case took place in Chicago in which fingerprints were used to convict Thomas Jennings of the murder of Clarence Hiller. There had been sparse evidence other than that the man's prints had been found at the scene of the crime. Such evidence had never been admitted in a capital case before. In a ruling at Jennings' last minute appeal on his murder conviction, the Illinois Supreme Court stated "…that there is a scientific basis for the system of finger print identification and that the courts are justified in admitting this class of evidence."

Chicago, with its history of political corruption, crime, scandal and vice, has also given us genus, creativity, humanism, industry and intellect. It is a city with big shoulders, deep pockets, a propensity for looking the other way, an extraordinarily excessive display of luxury and a disparity of economic equality, but fertile ground for ingenuity and unlimited possibility.

Come with me now to the Chicago of 1912, that fabled year of the Titanic, the Bull Moose Party, the South Pole expedition of Robert Falcon Scott, the Suffragettes, the Keystone Comedies, the chronicles of Tarzan, Piltdown Man, and, of course, the Unwritten Law.

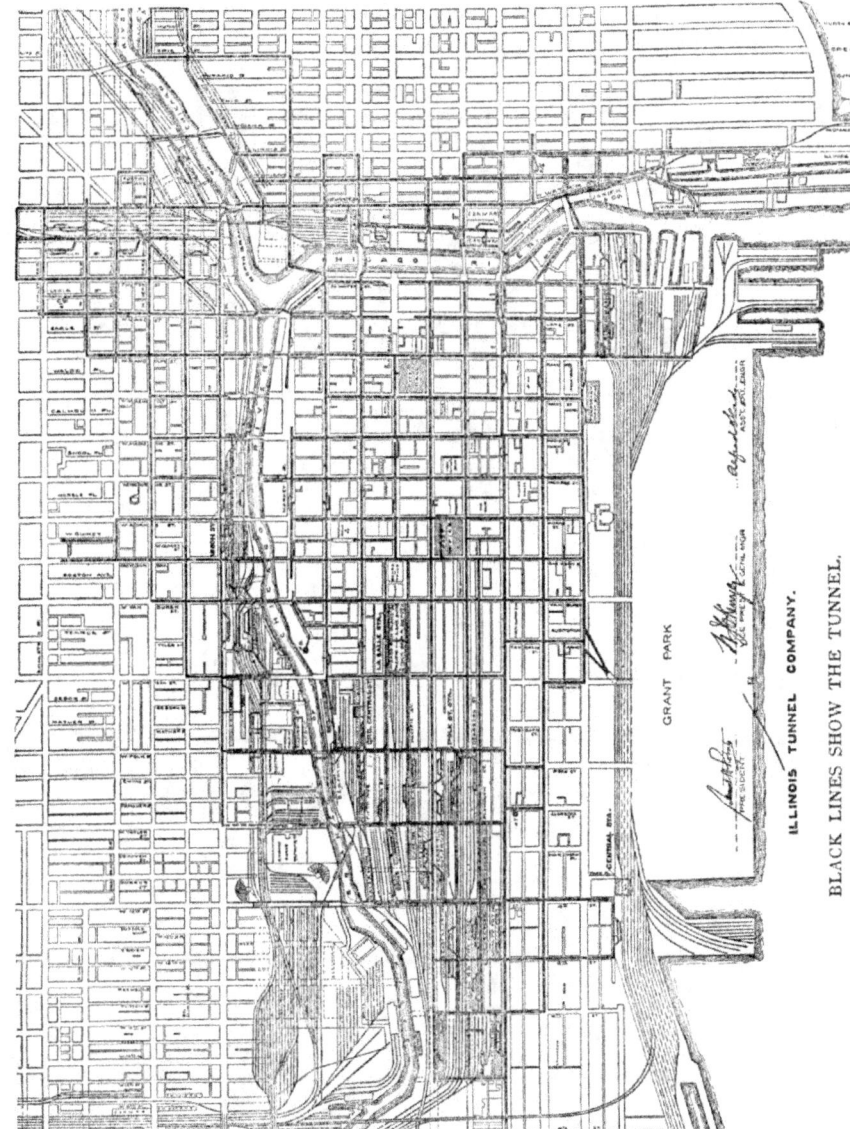

ILLINOIS TUNNEL COMPANY.

BLACK LINES SHOW THE TUNNEL.

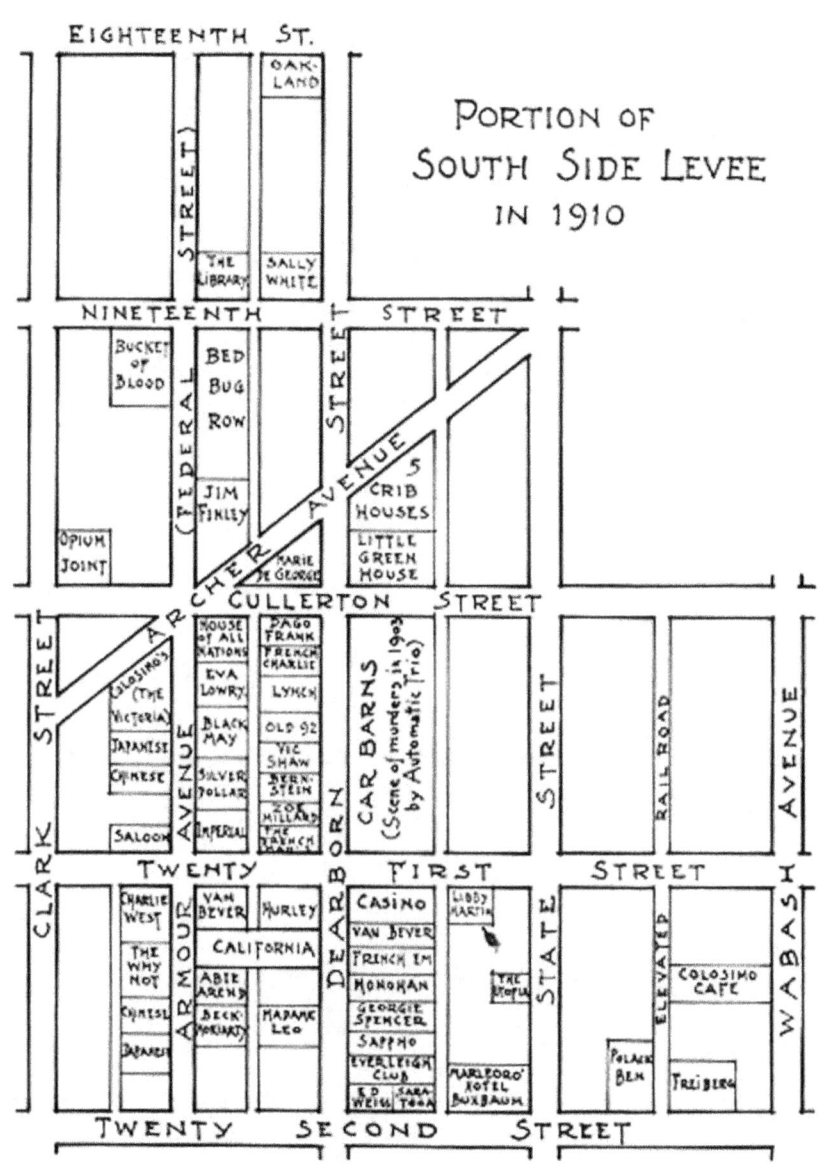

PORTION OF
SOUTH SIDE LEVEE
IN 1910

Byron Grush

1

The Jefferson League Club

I was born two years after the great fire so I don't remember the city as it was, its grandeur, its bustling downtown with those stately edifices much touted as the apex of architectural excellence—ultimately reduced to ashes. I have a somewhat vague recollection of the rebuilding...this, a mostly personal vision amplified by stories and anecdotes from my father. Father, you see, was in real estate. He was what I guess you would call a mogul of the times. Chicago was rebuilt upon the ashes of its destruction, with a new affirmation that carelessness would never again be part and parcel of its infrastructure. It would be proof against fire, but perhaps, not proof against graft.

Oh, I am not suggesting that my sainted father was dishonest; he did have a tendency to bribe certain politicians to obtain the rights to certain building sites. His real skill was in being able to anticipate where investing in the new growth would be most lucrative. In short, he became fabulously wealthy. Upon his death and the simultaneous death of my mother—this was due to a boating accident, a collision of their pleasure cruiser with an ore boat on Lake Michigan—I inherited a goodly sum, albeit one tied up in a trust fund which I was unable to access until I came of age.

I'd had odd jobs until that day of my twenty-first birthday. I worked as an errand boy at the Chicago Daily Times, and got to know some of the reporters...a group of ambitious and hard-working (and should I add, under-paid) men and one woman, who I looked up to, and who inspired some of my later endeavors...but I'm getting ahead of my story. I got a job with the Chicago Tunnel Company as an office boy (this will be seen as a pivotal element for this narrative, should you continue to read it). There were a few other uninteresting occupational escapades, but always jobs requiring little physical or intellectual effort on my part, and with just enough financial reward to scrape by. The house was taken care of by the trust, so that just left me responsible for meals...and entertainment.

By the time I could tap into the trust fund I was an expert at the art of drinking. My new stomping grounds were a district on the near south side called the Levee. And no, I did not partake of that other vice for which the Levee was so famous; I saw drinking companions enter the back rooms where the gambling tables were set up, and I watched as some climbed stairways to red-curtained cubicles where perfumed air and the muffled sounds of lust-making floated back down the rickety stairs—but no, I remained pure of heart, pure of body and pure of soul.

Why? I was just a frightened kid with little direction in life. But I did have one ambition: to find a world-shaking beauty of a woman, (one with the prerequisite pedigree), marry her, and carry on the legacy begun by my parents. That had been imprinted on my conscious mind nearly since infancy. That was an obsession that lurked at the threshold between the persona I believed was myself and that other entity, that unfulfilled, undiscovered self that had to struggle to emerge so as to abandon the shackles of my upbringing.

You might think me a prude, you might think me a snob, you might think me some kind of a fool. I was all of those. But perhaps it was all just a good excuse not to have to exert myself in a romantic direction. Perhaps it was the fear of success that kept me trapped in my inaction. While I waited for that perfect example of womanhood to appear, I began to assert myself in other ways.

I decided to become a freelance journalist. I was good with words, I was an able observer of events, and I could talk to people who might otherwise ignore me—because I was willing to listen. I wanted to travel, see the world, and, by reporting my experiences, have some small effect upon society. I wrote little blurbs that I submitted to the newspapers: the forced isolation of Typhoid Mary and her subsequent spreading of the disease, the spectacle of President Taft throwing out the first baseball on opening day, the near panic caused by the earth's passing through the tail of Halley's comet, the defeat of heavyweight boxing champion James Jeffries by the Negro, Jack Johnson and the following race riots.

I went to New York City to report on the Triangle Shirtwaist Factory Fire where 700 women, mostly immigrants, were trapped in the burning building...so many died that day! This article got me the attention I was seeking. I received an assignment to travel to Ciudad Juárez in Mexico where a revolution was taking place. But it was in Mexico City, as over 200 anti-Diaz demonstrators were massacred by government troops that my love affair with journalism finally soured. I returned to Chicago, disillusioned about the state of humanity, submitted my report, and resigned my temporary position with the Times. Was I withdrawing back into that shell that had imprisoned me for so many years? Or was I merely burned out, exhausted by the face of suffering and injustice the world had thrown at me?

I joined an exclusive gentlemen's club called the Jefferson League Club. I had to be sponsored by one of its members and voted on by the rest. There were some who thought me a bit of a vagabond, but ultimately, my father's reputation as one of the city's important developers got me through the process unscathed.

The Jefferson League Club occupied the top four floors of the Mason Building on Michigan Avenue at Randolph Street. The imposing edifice had been designed by Burnham and Root in the 1890s and had a heavy-looking red brick exterior and high-arched windows like monstrous browed eyes which gazed out toward the lake front that gave one a feeling of being transported back in time. The rooms included a dining area, suites where one could stay for as long as one's money held out, and a common room where the members could congregate to relax in overstuffed chairs and slip comfortably down behind unfolded newspapers. The furnishings and the décor imitated a cozy English country home. It was, of course, for members only.

It was there that I met and befriended Rodney Morton, who will figure prominently in this narrative.

Of Rodney Morton there is little I can tell. It was not so much that he was secretive about his background, it was just that he was expert at changing the subject when quizzed or asked to expand upon some reference he, I suppose inadvertently, slipped into the conversation. I can comment on my observations of this extraordinary and mysterious person, but these will be sparse owing to his fairly bland composure, his virtually blank countenance, and the neat but conservative costuming to which he was prone, and which gave few clues to his actual identity.

He was over fifty years of age, but how much over, I cannot say. He appeared to have retired from some essential position in the government or the military (although he had nothing in his manner of the bureaucratic)—I believed this because once or twice he was visited at the club by official looking persons who, although never in uniform, were straight-laced, orderly, and never looked one directly in the eye. He was methodical and took his time with things, even when it came to ordering a second brandy or preparing a cigar for smoking. This later action involved a ritual of rolling and snipping and licking that challenged one's patience, but increased one's admiration for the precision and dedication of the man for this, his preferred vice.

Rodney was a fan of puzzles…especially those involving real-life circumstances of a mysterious nature. Often we would analyze news items in the papers concerning interesting robberies or murders. One I recall that captivated the both of us for weeks was the case of the One-Legged Murderous Clown, as Charles Conway was called. Conway and his wife were circus performers and sometime con-artists. They had enticed a wealthy heiress from Baltimore named Sophie Singer and her fiancé to share their apartment in Chicago. Sophie ended up being strangled with the clown's handkerchief. The Conways left town with Sophie's jewelry. The fiancé discovered the body. Rodney postulated that although circumstantial evidence pointed to the Conways, it was entirely possible that the murder had been committed by the fiancé. I argued to the contrary and, as it turned out, the Conways were arrested, tried and convicted of the crime.

We were not opposed to fictional mysteries, in fact, we both read avidly the works of Arthur Conan Doyle: his Sherlock Holmes stories imbued with that terrific deductive (or was it inductive?) reasoning by the titular character. That there was a Chicago connection to the famed sleuth we had no doubt. One of Homes' arch opponents was the dastardly German agent, Von Bork. We knew from Watson's accounts that Holmes had tracked the vicious spy to America, beginning his quest in Chicago and following the trail to Buffalo and later to Skibbereen, posing as an Irish-American. Holmes certainly knew Teddy Roosevelt. (Roosevelt would be present for the Republican National Convention this coming June to be held at the Chicago Coliseum—I was excited to possibly see the great man.) Nebulous evidence about the Chicago/Homes connection perhaps, but when the impossible is eliminated, as Holmes would say, whatever remained, however improbable, must be the truth.

Usually, however, Rodney posed various invented scenarios with the object of stumping me. It became our favorite pastime, particularly on gray winter afternoons when our view from the club windows was obscured by thickening clouds portending of snow, or on inclement spring days when rain spattered against those same panes. One day in April of 1912, as we sat in our respective easy chairs at the Jefferson League Club, Rodney began to lay out one such scenario which would prove to have more significance for me than just that of being casual intellectual entertainment.

"The murder victim is slumped over his desk, a bullet hole in his forehead, a pool of blood spreading slowly on the green felt blotter on which he lies. The only door to the room is locked and bolted from the inside," said Rodney, setting his brandy on the occasional table next to his easy chair.

"You say 'murder victim?' Perhaps he committed suicide," I replied.

"No gun can be found in the room."

Rodney was fond of smacking down any explanation I could offer and would, as he did on this occasion, literally smack his hands down against his knees with a loud crack which no doubt disturbed the other denizens of our common room.

"He threw it out the window just before he collapsed," I retorted.

"The only window in the room is also bolted from the inside. There is no blood anywhere else except on the desk, so he did not move after he was shot. Besides, the ground outside the window has been searched and nothing found."

"The killer jumped out the window and rigged it to somehow bolt itself."

"No, there are no footprints in the ground under the window, and the ground is soft from a recent rain."

"The killer must have been hiding in the room and escaped after the murder was discovered."

"The room was thoroughly searched. No gun, no hiding places for a person or a weapon."

The exchange went on like this, with my brilliant logic dashed upon the rocks of reality…reality, that is, according to Rodney Morton.

"So it's impossible!" I said, stretching my legs out to rest upon the upholstered ottoman in front of me.

"That's the point. It is impossible to have happened that way, ergo, it didn't."

"What you're saying is that something you just described is false."

"Yes, something has to not be true in order for the murder victim to be found in the locked room in that manner. The mystery is, how was it done? Who did it, and why."

Rodney was fond of presenting me with riddles, piquing my curiosity, leading me through a maze of false clues and then thrusting upon me the obvious solution which, of course, never occurred to me. This time I was determined not to be outsmarted. I summoned Bruce, the club's waiter, and ordered a second brandy for Rodney and a Scotch for myself.

"Well, let's see," I began. "Either the man was murdered or he was not. If he committed suicide, then he had to have hidden the gun somewhere, which is impossible, therefore, he did not kill himself. Unless….he was poisoned!"

"What about the bullet wound?"

Rodney never gloated, outwardly. He did project an aura of cynicism when he knew he had the upper hand, but this was not a trait with which I could fault him. It was just his natural disdain of the rest of the world's inability to reason at the same pace and depth as he.

"Oh. Well," I said, "what if he was shot somewhere else and entered the room, wounded and about to die, closed and locked the door behind him, then sat down and died at his desk?"

"You forget," Rodney replied, "that the blood was found only on the desk."

"On the blotter!" I exclaimed. "Suppose he was shot, his head wrapped in the blotter so the blood would be contained, then he was placed in the room. That's why there was no gun found!"

"Still doesn't explain how the door got bolted from the inside."

Bruce appeared carrying a tray with our drinks. The congregating room of the Jefferson League Club was not crowded that afternoon, so our bizarre discussion wasn't bothering any of the other members. In fact, several bushy bearded old timers seemed mildly intrigued by the puzzle and I felt I might soon have help in solving it.

As Bruce served the drinks I asked him, "Bruce, if you wanted to kill somebody, how would you go about it?"

"Well sir, I would put poison in his drink," Bruce answered. Although there was a touch of irony in his response, I was circumspect in examining my Scotch. I noticed Rodney giving a wary eye to his brandy as well.

"Who found the body?" I quizzed.

"The maid had seen the man enter his study and close the door shortly after lunch. She heard a distinct click which she interpreted as the bolt being thrown. It was not unusual for him to lock himself in when he was engaged in certain of his work which was of a confidential nature. About two o'clock the mail had come and she knocked on the door to deliver his letters to him. When there was no response she tried the door and found it still locked. She became concerned and went for the man's son, who happened to be at home that day. He broke the door down but not until after several attempts which left him with a very sore shoulder, indeed. The jam was splintered as the door crashed open. Upon seeing his father slumped over the desk he immediately sent the maid for the police. There was an officer in the street outside who came promptly."

By now, three other club members had pulled their chairs into a tight circle around us, eagerly awaiting my conclusion. I looked from face to face, seeking encouragement but also feeling the pressure of my peers upon me to solve the mystery and score a point for…shall I say, our side? It was, after all, a game, perhaps not as exciting as, say, the Chicago Cubs verses St. Louis Cardinals, but definitely a game.

"I know! He was shot through the keyhole with a small caliber revolver." I could hardly contain my excitement at this novel solution. Would Rodney acknowledge my superior logic?

"The door had a Yale lock. It couldn't be done."

"Ah…then the door was simply locked from the outside after the killer left."

"No...the door was also bolted, with one of those sliding bolts. The door jam splintered when the son broke it down."

It was time for drastic speculation:

"But the son was alone in the room for a brief period while the maid went for the policeman. He could have taken the gun away. And there could have been an accomplice who was hiding in the room who he then let escape."

"The maid would have seen someone else in the room. She did not."

"Maybe she was in on it!"

"Oh come now, why would the maid want to help murder her employer? Besides which, the policeman was there within minutes. The son would not have had time to remove and conceal the gun somewhere else. You haven't got it!"

Rodney's hands smacked loudly against his knees. I was hoping that it hurt as badly as it sounded.

"No, and I guess I'll have to pay for the drinks today," I said, and gave a disparaging glace at our kibitzers as if to say, a lot of help you've been!

2

Connie Dunning

The following morning saw me again in the common room of the Jefferson League Club, conversing with Rodney about various news items, including the loss of the Scott Expedition to the South Pole and the prospects for Alaska to become a United States Territory. The country was growing by leaps and bounds, with the two new states of New Mexico and Arizona recently added. Chicago now boasted a population of well over two million people! Surely it could accommodate no more.

Eventually, of course, we returned to Rodney's locked room mystery. I was running out of ideas and ready to solicit the solution from Rodney. "Well, I confess," I said, "that I am at a loss as to how the murder was committed." I was about to demand the answer from him when Bruce tapped my shoulder and spoke in a lowered voice: "Sir, there is a young lady asking for you in the lobby."

The Jefferson League Club, being a gentlemen-only club, did not allow women past the lobby entrance. Were it up to me I would have welcomed an occasional visit from the fairer sex if only as a foil to the stuffiness and tedium fostered by our exclusive environment. I excused myself, petitioning Rodney not to reveal the answer until I returned, and descended the broad, curving staircase. The statuesque beauty who awaited me was dressed elegantly in silken tunic and hobble skirt (I always marveled at how women could walk in those tight dresses). She wore a large wide-brimmed hat topped with an ostrich feather which she was adjusting to a seductive tilt as I approached. That hat reminded me of the recent news we'd had only just this April of the Titanic sinking; it was similar to one worn in a photo of Titanic survivor, Margaret Brown, the woman they called "The Unsinkable."

The Titanic! No one could believe this great behemoth of a passenger ship, the world's largest, this unsinkable luxury liner on her maiden voyage, could have disappeared beneath the waves of the North Sea so suddenly, taking with her 1,500 people! The celebrities were mourned, of course: John Jacob Astor IV, Benjamin Guggenheim, Isidor Straus, Archibald Butt, and others—but the passengers in steerage, the noble crew members who stayed with the ship, the many who were unable to find a seat on a lifeboat—these were the tragic losses that shocked and dismayed us all when the pitifully small number of 708 survivors reached New York via the RMS Carpathia.

I shook the thought from my mind and reached a welcoming hand out to the young woman.

"Connie!" I exclaimed. "It's wonderful to see you."

Connie was Constance Dunning, daughter of my former employer, Willard Herbert Dunning, who was the manager and major stock holder of the Chicago Tunnel Company. Dunning was the brilliant entrepreneur who had turned an underground electric railway which had been built to install telephone cabling beneath the city into a sixty-mile long freight system.

Few of the Loop-dwellers who worked in the many buildings in Chicago's busy business district were aware of that vast underground labyrinth of tunnels that had been excavated there beginning in 1899. The Illinois Telephone and Telegraph Company laid their cables throughout the city by virtue of these subterranean passageways and had built over 26 miles of tunnels through which a narrow gauge railway ran to facilitate the work. The tunnels were eventually expanded to a linear distance of 60 miles and began being used to deliver freight between the various substations and the basements of downtown buildings. The Chicago Tunnel Company, Willard Dunning's brainchild, was the concern currently operating the tunnel system.

Dunning had originally hired me as an office boy but upon learning of my blossoming literary talent (I had begun dabbling in freelance writing by then and was somewhat of a braggart around the office about my abilities), wanted me to write copy for the promotion of his freight line. To do so, he required that I should ride along on one of the engines in order to get an idea of the tunnel's scope. I didn't relish the idea of being 40 feet below the surface of Chicago in a six-foot wide cavern and so I had declined. Thus I was to leave the service of the Chicago Tunnel Company, but not before the radiant and angelic beauty, Connie Dunning, came into my life.

I had met the boss's daughter, Connie, one afternoon when both of us happened to converge upon her father's office for different reasons. I was immediately struck by her attractiveness and decided there and then to pursue her. I have mentioned how I was "saving myself" for the perfect woman…and here was a likely candidate: serenely beautiful, sweet by nature, and a future heiress!

Connie had chestnut locks piled high in the latest fashion. Not one curl escaped to caress her cheek or nape; she was as immaculate about coiffeur and costume as she was careful about her deportment (was it grace, or just good practice?) I was, as I have said, taken with her. Her soft tones and careful phrases made conversation delightful, although somewhat lacking in the fire and exuberance of those others of her ilk…those society maidens who came out formally, and then partied all night in the "modern" manner.

She was knowledgeable and had traveled abroad. Any young man would be enchanted by her and revel in her companionship. I was cautious in my approach; you handle a delicate flower with care. I wasn't in love with her: that would come later I supposed. But as I delved more deeply into her thoughts and emotions during our lengthy conversations, I became aware of a slightly darker side to her personality. The most miniscule of incidents from her childhood, which she recited only after my insistent probing, seemed to suggest a certain morbidity; a fascination for dead things. It was her story of a deceased pet, a blue-gray, yellow-eyed Chartroux—just a kitten, really—that she had kept in a shoebox under her bed long after its death, that led me to surmise there was more to this flower than its fragrance.

We had taken many a long walk through Lincoln Park but as yet had failed to cement a much stronger bond than that of sincere friendship and mutual regard. Perhaps she was too aloof or I was too restrained—we made quite a pair. One day as we lingered by the lagoon, I pressed her for her feelings. "I am not ready for marriage," she answered, "and any courting I do would be disingenuous. I treasure your friendship, but…"

I had nearly given up hope of establishing a foothold into the Dunning dynasty; those plans had fallen neatly into my obsession with the continuation of my own family's legacy, as unethical as that may seem. I still admired Connie dearly, and would have relished a romance, but it was not to be. Now she stood before me looking distraught and anguished.

"What is the matter, Connie?" I asked.

"It's Peter. Peter has disappeared!" came her answer in a voice that wavered and broke.

Peter Dunning was Constance's brother, younger by two years, whom she had nurtured and guarded throughout their childhood. What I knew of Peter, other than Connie's fondness for him, was that he was inclined toward a rakish and risky deportment, often necessitating his rescue by someone from the family, usually Connie.

Once Peter, only twelve years of age, had taken one of the family automobiles for a "joyride" (as it is called by today's youth). This episode ended abruptly with the vehicle flattened against an ancient oak, not more than two blocks from the Dunning mansion. Another time Peter had attempted to cross Lake Michigan, appropriating a small sail boat which been moored, but not locked, at Diversey Harbor. The Coast Guard returned him home and Father Dunning had to pull strings to keep him out of jail.

And here was Connie, once the object of my affections, now a dear friend, troubled by some new escapade by her brother, Peter. I could not help but respond to those dark, dejected eyes—the spell they cast had captured my soul long ago, and now they implored me, begged me for succor. "Please sit down. Tell me about it," I suggested.

"No," she answered. "Please take me home. I'll tell you on the way." She turned to leave. I could do nothing but follow.

I called for my car to be brought around while I collected hat, gloves and walking stick. I had recently purchased an Overland model 38 Roadster with a cherry red finish and double set of running lamps. It was a four-seater with an eight valve inline engine that promised to do about 40 miles per hour on the open road. As we were only motoring a short way to Wrightwood Avenue where the Dunning residence was, I wouldn't get an opportunity to show off the engine's prowess. I helped Connie step up into the automobile and in a few minutes we were puttering up Michigan Avenue.

I was in no hurry as Connie's company, even considering her present distress, was like money in the bank for an impoverished romantic such as myself. I jogged over to the Outer Drive which is now called Lake Shore Drive (or as some called it, Potter Palmer's driveway). This broad Boulevard ran along the lakefront all the way to Fullerton Avenue. We passed the Palmer mansion...a castle if ever there was one. I had heard it cost over a million dollars to build in 1883. To me it represented a mishmash of styles from Gothic to Romanesque to Italianate. It had turrets and minarets and a glass dome and loomed three stories above Lake Shore Drive. One could imagine German soldiers armed with cross bows peering from its ramparts.

It was pleasant, driving along with horse drawn carriages and the occasional auto which would honk an enthusiastic greeting at us. Young trees, I suppose maples or elms, lined the west side of the road along the broad sidewalk while white-capped waves were clearly visible to the east. Connie had wrapped a scarf around her face against the wind which buffeted us in the open roadster so I leaned closer to her in order to hear her story.

"Peter has been seeing a girl up by Mount Pleasant...what they used to call Ducktown. Father has been furious. They'd been at odds with each other anyway because Peter doesn't want to join the business. And now he has this girl. Anyway, he disappeared last Monday. Didn't show up for dinner, which, as you know, is a cardinal sin with Father. We think he may have run off with this woman...girl...a Pole, mind you. Her people work at the steel mill!"

"Ducktown...isn't that near the Bubbly Creek?" I said, more of a statement than a question.

Bubbly Creek was what they called the South Branch of the Chicago River, which ran between Bridgeport and McKinley Park. Gas bubbles rose to the surface from the decomposing offal and bloody animal parts thrown into the river by meat packers, hence the descriptive name. Originally a wetland, the area had been dredged and drained and the creek took the flow off into the Chicago River.

Simultaneously, the reclaimed land was inhabited and the creek became a sewer for the Union Stock Yards and others who threw the unusable remnants of pigs, cattle and sheep into it. Barrels of entrails and buckets of blood found their way into that slowly moving cesspool of a stream. Methane and hydrogen sulfide from the decomposing gore bubbled and even occasionally caught fire.

"Ducktown is in the old swampy section," Connie answered. "There are houses up on stilts! People don't like living there, but their work is where the mills are. Peter told us all about it. He complained about the conditions as if the disgraceful circumstances of those people were somehow our fault... can you imagine?"

"Sounds like Peter has strayed away from your family values. Is he a reformer? Votes for women, that sort of thing?"

"He disdains class distinctions. Takes on causes all the time. I don't think Women's Suffrage is actually one of them, though. And, I think he likes provoking Father by taking a liberal stance and throwing it in his face. The other day he actually said he admired the struggles of the working classes to form unions. That certainly got Father's goat! "

"Did he say anything before he disappeared? Leave a note?"

"Come in when we get home and I'll show you what he left for me." Connie was silent for the remaining trip.

At North Avenue, the Drive encounters Lincoln Park and merges with Clark Street, becoming the park's western border. I sensed that Connie's irritation precluded a stroll through that wonderful place with its verdant expanse of trees, lake and parade grounds. I would have to be content with memories of previous excursions. After turning west on Fullerton Avenue I jogged north on Lake View. This took me to the idyllic, tree-line street of Wrightwood where Connie resided with her parents and sibling.

We turned onto Wrightwood and I parked in front of the Dunning mansion, a strange conglomeration of German Baroque and French Rococo styles with a smattering of Greek Revivalism. Two life-sized statues stood as pillars at the main entrance: one of Pan draped in a wreath of grapes and grape leaves, and the other of a buxom Aphrodite in a pose that would be acceptable in a Paris salon, but was a bit risqué for Chicago. Opulence was the operative word at the Dunning mansion. Inside were more pillars, not figurative, but marble struck through with ruby colored veins. A tiled hall with a vaulted ceiling led to a more sedate sitting room containing a few upholstered chairs scattered willy-nilly as if they had moved around under their own volition in a surreal game of musical chairs. We sat.

Connie produced a folded paper from her small handbag. She handed it to me and I read what her brother had written in a cramped script that wandered across the page like the spore of some frightened animal:

Dearest Constance,

You of all people I do not wish to hurt. You must understand that Mother and Father don't get me. Especially Father who makes me so angry sometimes that I wish he were dead! There, I've said it. I am involved with the loveliest and sweetest person on God's earth! They can't accept it. I must do what I must do. Please don't think ill of me.

Your loving brother, Peter.

"You think he has run off with this woman? He doesn't actually say what it is he 'must do.' "

"I think so."

"What can I do to help?"

"Find him and bring the little bastard back, dammit!" This booming retort came from behind us. I turned and saw there the lofty figure of Willard Dunning, master of his castle, but head of a sadly dysfunctional family, or so it seemed. I stood, as if in the presence of royalty, and nodded obediently. Such was the commanding presence of this dynamic and extraordinary individual.

Did I sense that even Connie was in awe of this man...perhaps in a small way afraid of him? Certainly her body language indicated it as she now stiffened and the color drained from her face. At the time I believed I may have imagined this, but because of later events...well, there I go again, getting ahead of my story.

Willard Herbert Dunning was tall, which contributed to his dominating demeanor. At well over six feet one *had* to look up to him. This he took for granted. His sense of privilege was apparent and, perhaps, deserved, that is if one valued ruthless capitalism and self-centered empire building. Dunning bragged that he was one of those self-made men who had forged a great industrialized nation out of the wilderness—of course that wasn't true. He had built his fortune on the basis of inherited money.

15

Dunning's father, a true pioneer, had emigrated from Ireland during the great Potato Famine. He had survived the hardships of poverty and discrimination and managed to feed his family by pushing a cart of fresh vegetables along the unpaved streets of Chicago. The Great Fire destroyed the tenement they had lived in. Cormac Dunning became a rag picker. With money thus earned, the irrepressible Irishman bought cheaply made clothing and began peddling it out of a store front he shared with a shoemaker. The business grew and a decade later, Dunning's Dry Goods had expanded into a mini-empire of three stores, covering the south, west and north sides of the city. By the time his son, Willard, came of age, there was ample financing available for his own foraging into the business world.

Willard did not start at the bottom, learning his way, as had his father. Willard simply bought existing businesses, ones that had faltered due to inept management…and he got them at bargain prices. A company called the Calumet Dredging Company was absorbed into the Dunning conglomerate and soon Dunning was at work deepening the Illinois and Michigan Canal in an attempt to reverse the flow of the Chicago River. This was unsuccessful, but it afforded Dunning with many important contacts within the political establishment of the Windy City. When Chicago's Sanitary District installed canal locks to finally reverse the flow in 1900, Dunning's company was right there, digging what would be called the Chicago Sanitary and Ship Canal, to collect Lake Michigan water and hasten the cleanup of the so called Stinking River. And now he ran the Chicago Tunnel Company.

What would it have been like, I wondered, for Connie and her brother, growing up in a household ruled by this self-absorbed and powerful man? I had had some little contact with him when I worked in his office, and I knew him to be a megalomaniac, a harsh task master, a man whose vocabulary didn't include the phrase, "I can't." Connie seldom alluded to her father during our conversations. I did surmise, however, that her mother had little influence over domestic issues, and could only provide the role model of an obedient, subservient marital partner for Connie. Perhaps this helped explain Connie's reluctance to engage in the romantic adventure I had wished to pursue with her.

"I'll find the…Peter," I found myself saying. "I'll convince him to return home."

At this, Willard Dunning's stern gaze hardly wavered. He gave the slightest of nods, then turned on his heel and exited the room. It was as if an audience with the Pope had just concluded.

"Come," said Connie, "I'll walk you to your car."

Once outside the great mansion I felt the release of the tension that had built so abruptly after only a few words from Dunning. A light breeze ruffled the maple leaves. I had the bizarre notion that one of the statues guarding the mansion's front door had just winked at me. I looked deeply into Connie's eyes and gave her what I calculated would be a reassuring smile. "I'll find him for you," I told her.

"Yes, do find him. See that he is not endangering himself in some fool-hardy way. Talk to him, tell him I am on his side. But tell him...tell him *not* to come home just now. I'm afraid of what father might do."

"Might do? Why are you afraid of your father, Connie? Has he ever..."

"It's just that Peter is such a sensitive boy. Father will certainly light into him...not physically, of course. I didn't mean that. But Father has such a temper..."

"All right, Connie. You have my word. I'll find Peter. And I won't bring him home...not at this juncture. If he's with this girl..."

"Yes," Connie said, "*if* he's with a girl..."

3

Ducktown

Mount Pleasant, an ironic name for a place better represented by its nickname, Ducktown, lay in the fetid crotch of the confluence of the west and south forks of the South Branch of the Chicago River. To the north were the iron and steel mills and brickyards that gave employment to the area's residents. To the south was the infamous Bubby Creek and beyond, the packing houses where an attempt was made to use almost every part of the cattle and pigs processed there—the unused parts were thrown in the creek. This resulted in coating of the banks of the river with dried blood and hair and a gruesome tide of entrails and other nasty bits that floated down stream.

I had taken Connie's plea to heart and scheduled the day for a trip to Ducktown with the hope that the single clue I had to Peter's whereabouts, the girl he was seeing, would hasten the fruition of my quest. Cherchez la femme, as the French say. Look for the woman. There is another expression, an over-used cliché about trying to find a needle in a haystack. But Connie had given me an address she had found, she told me, on an envelop pushed to the back of Peter's dresser drawer. This address would be a good place to start my investigation.

Although haste was indicated, I could not resist the opportunity to drive along the banks of this decrepit drainage and see for myself what the legends had painted as grim and disgusting. Would I see great expanding rings of the foulest muck and mire? Little wisps of blue flame from exploding methane bubbles? I wondered if I would encounter any of the scavengers I had heard about who drifted through the sludge in low rowboats scraping the surface up for the purpose of producing lard which they would sell to unsuspecting housewives or restaurants wishing to cut costs.

I stopped near a dead willow tree whose gray-white skeletal branches drooped no longer toward the water source, but away from it, as if the tree had died during an attempt to escape from the filth. I walked to the very edge of the creek, using my walking stick for stability against the slippery dirt. I was at a narrow, funnel tip from the main pool, and I was very glad I was far away from its morbid source. Before me ran a fetid, glistening, ribbon of indeterminable hue; a malignant scar across the soggy landscape which defied any sense that its origin was human.

It depressed me greatly, seemed to beckon—as if demons from some unknown circle of Hell writhed within it, used it to enter the land of the living and suck from the good and the sane any semblance of hope or happiness, like a vampire sucking the blood of its victims. The spirits of the dead animals...hundreds, thousands...millions of innocent creatures, bludgeoned to near death, their throats slit, their bodies torn to pieces and hung from hooks while their remaining life's fluids dripped onto the floor, ran through troughs, and splashed into the great sewer of Bubbly Creek...these spirits haunted the place. I found I was gagging. Phlegm caught in my throat. I had to leave that horrible sight and so I scrambled up the bank to the Overland.

Once I entered the cluster of dwellings known as Ducktown, the houses I saw did seem to be raised on stilts. Piles of brick or wooden pylons were sunk into the swampy earth so that ground water wouldn't seep through the floor boards. Houses made of weathered wood, with nary a scrap of paint to be seen sat graying in the smog issuing from the mills. When the wind shifted, a rancid, throat-choking odor of dead, dying and decaying animals, mixed with the acrid fumes from the foundries assailed the denizens of Ducktown—and now enveloped my otherwise hopeful outlook with a dismal dread.

The streets here were still unpaved and one wondered what vile elements were mixed into the dirt and horse-droppings and randomly discarded garbage. I dearly hoped no nail or spike lay buried there that might puncture my tires…the prospect of having to change a flat concerned me greatly. My once shiny roaster was now splattered with mud and worse as I pulled up to the address Connie had given me. A house like all the others, it resembled a barn or a stable more than a dwelling made for humans.

I climbed creaking stairs and knocked with my walking stick, although I was afraid my pounding might dislodge the door from its hinges. A space appeared as the door swung open ever so slightly, and in that space appeared a pair of dark eyes sunk in a mélange of dirt, dried food, snot and drool. When I was finally able to identify this apparition as a face, one belonging to an urchin clothed in ragged shirt and pants coated with the same sticky mixture, I said, "Son, is your mother at home?"

The urchin shook his head: no. "Your father?" I asked. Again, his non-verbal answer was no. I knew better than to ask his name. I would no doubt receive a shrug or a door slammed in my face. The boy stared blankly at me, then his gaze shifted past me to the roadster. "Do you like that car?" I asked. "Would you like to come out and see it up close?" He nodded, an elfish grin forming under the crust that covered his countenance.

I led him to where the Overland was parked; pointed out the head lamps and the great wooden spokes of the wheels. I flipped open the hood and let him examine the engine, which seemed to delight him more than if I had offered him cotton candy or ice cream wrapped in a waffle. I let him sit in the driver's seat, although the patina that would be transferred from his dirty overalls to my leather seats gave me pause. His grin broadened as he worked the steering wheel back and forth. I was just happy his feet didn't reach the floor boards...and the gas pedal!

"Now, son, again...where is your mother?"

"She took the baby to the park," came his reply.

The park? Ah, yes, the park. There was usually a swatch of land which was reserved for the recreation and enjoyment of nature for the local residents in various parts of the city. I had to wonder, when did these people have time for recreation? But of course, my low opinion of the working classes was ill conceived...the result of my own youth, wasted in the velvet pursuit of laziness and leisure. This acute view of the pitiful state of the struggling poor (why don't they pull themselves up by their bootstraps?) would dissipate as I became acquainted with at least one of the denizens of Ducktown. That happens later in my story, so for now, think of me unkindly if you will. It is of little consequence.

McKinley Park, which was the nearest nature area to Ducktown, was a 25 acre track of land south of where we stood, named after President McKinley who was felled by an anarchist's bullet some dozen years ago. It was no small place, having a lagoon, a swimming pool, a children's playground and a ballpark, not to mention walking paths winding through hazelnut trees and stone pillars. How would I ever be able to locate the mother of this ragamuffin?

"Come with me, boy," I said. "Shove over. You'll have to show me where she is." And so the grubby ruffian slid across to the passenger side smiling broadly. I noted, a bit nervously, that he observed the starting procedures I applied to the auto: the turning of the magneto switch, the opening of the throttle, the cranking of the engine (which necessitated my climbing out of the automobile and leaving the child alone within reach of the gear shift!) I returned to the driver's seat, gunned the engine, and popped out the clutch risking embedding the wheels into the soft dirt of the road, but I knew this was the thrill of a lifetime for the lad.

Once we reached McKinley Park he led me to the children's playground where a woman sat, babe in arms, watching the older children play. The park was a stark contrast to the depressing squalor we had just left. Somehow, by virtue of public works, the city had created a gem of natural beauty to offset the blight and, most likely, to ease its conscience. A gentle wind blew across the lagoon and rustled the fir trees surrounding the playground: a hushed whisper that seemed to say, "all is right with the world." Children frolicked on teeter-totters and climbed jungle-gyms as if the reality of their world didn't exist. I approached the woman.

She was younger than I had expected, dressed neatly in a smock that was obviously old, but not yet worn out. A red babushka was tied under her chin framing a once pretty face with a few worry lines and a pair of sad blue eyes. She sat, cradling the infant in her arms on a wooden bench with peeling green paint; the baby carriage was parked along side. When she saw me accompanied by her son, she looked startled. "Stephen, what is this?" she asked.

"Excuse me, Ma'am," I said. "Your son has been kind enough to bring me here to you. I am a friend of Peter Dunning, who I think your daughter knows. I am trying to locate him and I wonder if you can help me."

Here followed one of those long, uncomfortable moments as the woman studied me. She must have been evaluating the consequences of remaining mute versus opening up to me. It was natural to be suspicious of strangers. And this one (myself) had mentioned her daughter. And this one had her son in tow. She glanced over at Stephen, who still was smiling from the thrilling motorcar ride I just given him. Perhaps this softened her resolve a bit. She looked back at me and spoke:

"Peter...yes, that's Alicia's friend. I know him."

"You see, we think they may have run off somewhere together."

"My Alicia? Oh, no. She's a good girl. She wouldn't do that."

"Have you seen her recently?"

"This morning, before she left for work. She's a good girl, I tell you."

The baby began to fuss...apparently sensing its mother's anxiety. The woman wrapped the infant snuggly in a woolen shawl which had lain across her lap. This seemed to placate the creature.

"Of course she is a good girl," I returned. "Can you tell me where I can find her? Perhaps she knows Peter's whereabouts. It would help me tremendously!"

She paused to consider this. After all, she didn't know me from Adam and had no reason to trust me. The boy, Stephen, plopped down next to her on the bench. I said, "His family is very worried about him. If Alicia can help..."

"Okay, she works at Marshall Field's store downtown. A very good job has my girl! In the shipping and receiving."

She now placed her arm around her son Stephen. I wondered at this strong woman, raising children in this dismal environment. She had a daughter who was apparently of working age, a son of perhaps 8 or 10 years, and a new baby, all to feed and clothe and worry over. I too was beginning to soften. And then this from the woman:

"Stephen, when you get home you tell that no good brother of yours to get off his duff and look for a job!"

So there was one more child in this menagerie! And the husband? Working in one of the mills, I supposed. My picture of this family was one of constant struggle, daily suffering. It was all so foreign to my experience and my vision of how society should be. How would these people ever get ahead on the wages they were paid? And the young boy, would he be working in the mill one day soon? I knew there was some kind of national movement to abolish child labor, but so far no progress toward that goal had been accomplished. Children, especially those of disadvantaged families, were sent to work in textile mills or in the fields instead of going to school. We were becoming a nation of the extremely wealthy and the extremely impoverished— rapidly diverging classes—and the uneducated poor had no chance of bettering themselves.

I hoped my newly found angst didn't show as I looked at the woman. I leaned closer to examine the babe on her lap. It was bright pink against the dull brown shawl, and cooed as if it were a bird in the nest. The hope of new life in a hostile environment—my God! I was getting depressed. "That's a sweet thing," I said if only to alleviate my own dark mood.

"She's just six months now. Her name is Bernice. We had hoped for another boy, but…"

"I'm sure she'll be a blessing to you." Here, I thought of offering the woman some money. I had plenty. But all at once I knew that would be a grievous error. She had her pride and no doubt was far more adept at survival than I would be in her circumstances. So I merely said:

"I have to thank you, Mrs…"

"Kaminski."

"Mrs. Kaminski. May I offer you a ride back home?"

"No, I enjoy the walk. I have the buggy."

"Well, I can at least give Stephen a ride. I'm sure he'd like that."

The boy, Stephen, jumped up and said, "Can I look at your cane?" My walking stick featured a silver lion's head at its top. This had apparently fascinated the boy. I handed it to him. The sudden movement precipitated the flight of a flock of starlings from a nearby maple tree. Stephen raised my walking stick up to his shoulder as if it were a rifle and took aim at the birds. "Bang! Bang! Bang!" he exclaimed.

And I, in a great leap of insight, uttered, "Of course!" I believed I now knew exactly how the locked room murder had been committed! It may seem incongruous that, as I was involved with the search for Peter Dunning and far removed from the Jefferson Club where there was both the leisure time and the necessity (to avert boredom) of dabbling in trivial mysteries, that I should suddenly fix on this locked room business again. But the use of the walking stick as a rifle by the boy had stimulated my unconscious mind. I had made a connection which upon reflection seems absurd, but which none the less prompted a new theory. I would have to find Rodney and report the solution. Oh, how I would gloat.

But first I would find Alicia Kaminski. And I still had to locate Peter Dunning. I had a real life mystery to solve and I had made a promise to Connie.

When we returned to the Kaminski house a thought occurred to me. "Do you suppose," I asked Stephen, "that your brother might be home? I would like to ask him what he knows about Peter Dunning, the man I'm searching for."

Stephen was noncommittal as usual. He merely shrugged. I followed him through the doorway into an abode that startled me. I don't know what I had expected: dirty carpets, balls of dust caught up in cat fur or the like, bits of discarded food, stacks of old newspapers, all the jetsam of a depressed and under privileged lifestyle. But before me was a room that might have leaped from the pages of a magazine! A cozy, warm and tidy room—not elegant in its furnishings, but immaculate in its order and cleanliness. Spotless antimacassars were draped on the backs of two well-used, overstuffed easy chairs. Lace curtains hung to floor length at the front windows; the glass panes were pristine...too bad the view was so ugly. A vase of fresh-picked flowers sat on a low table before a sofa covered with a hand-made quilt. There was a bookshelf which displayed framed pictures of an elderly man and woman in what appeared to be peasant garb standing in front of an ancient church, no doubt somewhere in Poland, and newer pictures of the Kaminsky children...the two boys and the girl were obviously much younger when these were taken. The girl was very pretty; I wondered what she would look like now.

"So, Stephen...no big brother?"

"Nope. He ain't here."

"He *isn't* here."

"That's what I said."

The boy motioned for me to follow him and led me into the kitchen. Here again I perceived order and cleanliness. If I had expected to see a dirty pot thrown haphazardly into the sink or a reeking trash bin full of a week's garbage, I was pleasantly disappointed. Pots and pans were hung from hooks. A shelf contained shiny plates and glassware. A small table stood at the center of the room, covered with a green and white checked table cloth. Stephen wandered to the icebox and opened it. "Lemonade?" he asked. I declined.

We sat at the kitchen table and talked. As Stephen slurped his lemonade, I quizzed him about his life here in Ducktown. "Do you go to school?" I asked.

"It's summer," he complained.

"I know, but will you go to school in the fall? Do you like it?"

"I go. But I hate it! They make me do arithmetic. Ugh!"

"Stephen, arithmetic is very important. Especially if you want to make something of yourself in this life."

"I won't need no numbers at the mill."

"I hope you would not end up at the mill, son. You can be anything you want to be...but you must get a good education. Here, let us suppose you are the manager of a grocery store. You have two piles of fruit. One is of apples and there are exactly 27 apples in the pile. The other is of bananas and it contains 32 bananas. Now, how many bananas would you have to take away to make the two piles equal?"

"See, that's exactly the kind of problem I hate! That's why I don't like school."

"But what is the answer? How would you make the two piles equal?"

"I would just start eating bananas until the piles looked about the same."

I had to laugh. "A creative solution involving visual acuity. Perhaps you will grow up to be an artist." Stephen just gave me his characteristic blank stare.

"Well, it's time for me to go." I took his hand and shook it. "It's been a pleasure meeting you, young sir. I want you to be sure to mind your parents and stay in school." I might have been the most condescending adult the boy had ever met, but I truly hoped he would take what I had said to heart. The morning was waning, and I had to drive downtown to find Alicia Kaminsky. I was tempted to stop at the Jefferson League Club to inform Rodney of my new theory, but duty called. And so I returned to the Overland and made my way to State Street where the department store, Marshall Field and Company, was located.

4

Marshall Field & Company

The history of Marshall Field & Company is intrinsically linked with the history of the city of Chicago itself. In 1852, a young man named Potter Palmer opened a dry goods store at 137 Lake Street in Chicago's business district—same Potter Palmer whose castle-like mansion now stands on Lake Shore Drive. Potter Palmer and Company became the most successful establishment of its kind in the Midwest, primarily by catering to women and adopting a policy of returns with no questions asked. A few years later, a then 21 year old Marshall Field moved to Chicago from Pittsfield, Massachusetts. Field found employment with another dry goods firm, but by 1865, he and a friend, Levi Leiter, had become partners with Palmer and the store became Field, Palmer, Leiter & Company.

Field and Leiter bought out Palmer, whose failing health had led him to enter the "less stressful" business of real estate. Palmer leased his new, six-story building on the corner of State and Washington, known as the "Marble Palace," to the partners and the store became Field & Leiter. On October 8, 1871, most of the business district burned to the ground in the Great Chicago Fire. Field had managed to salvage some of his merchandise and soon reopened in an unburned building at Madison and Market Streets.

Field and Leiter later moved into a new building at State and

Washington, but in 1877, fire swept through the store destroying their business for a second time. Of course they rebuilt and in fact, expanded. Leiter sold out to Field in 1881, and the firm became what we now know as Marshall Field and Company. A young man named Harry Selfridge worked for Field for nearly 25 years. He was a gifted promoter and coined the phrase "Only [so many] Shopping Days Until Christmas," and "The Customer is Always Right." He went on to found Selfridge's Department Store on Oxford Street in London.

The Marshall Field Retail store on State Street now occupied nearly an entire city block, having grown since the Great Fire by the purchase and destruction of adjacent buildings in order to expand Field's real estate holdings. In fact, they were now in the process of demolishing a 16 story skyscraper and building an annex so as to dominate the whole block. They were calling it the world's largest department store. Standing in the open central atrium and gaping up five stories at the Tiffany mosaic glass dome, one would certainly agree.

I took the stairway from the granite floored entrance to the lower level where the shipping room was buzzing with activity. Men and women carried wire baskets filled with the smaller packages while hand trucks were being used to move the larger goods. All the employees were clothed in black uniforms. My task to find Alicia Kaminski was going to be difficult. I loitered, which caused curious looks from the workers and probably would eventually result in my expulsion from the area. I spotted a fellow holding a clip board and ventured to inquire of him if a Miss Kaminski was present. Employees were not permitted visitors during working hours, I was told. Could he get a message to her that I was waiting to see her, I enquired, slipping a fiver into the man's hand. He could and would.

As I waited in the shipping room, I happened to notice someone scrutinizing me near the back of the room where a freight elevator was located. I recognized him at once—it was Peter Dunning! As I began to move toward him, he slipped into the elevator, pulled up the wooden gate, and set it motion. Down! Where in the world was it going, I wondered? We were already on the lowest level of the building.

"It goes to the freight tunnels," said a voice as I stood, open-mouthed, staring down the shaft and watching serpentine steel cables uncoiling and the huge counter weight climbing upward. I turned to see a young woman, dressed in black, golden hair sequestered in a hair net, blue eyes sparkling. "My supervisor said you wanted to see me," she said.

"Are you Alicia Kaminski?"

"Yes sir, I am."

"You know Peter Dunning?"

"That was Peter who went down the elevator just now."

"Yes, I know. I wonder if I could talk to you about him somewhere…more private."

"I can take a break for lunch at the end of the hour. I could meet you in the employees' cafeteria."

We agreed to meet later. As I had some time to kill, I turned back to the elevator, pushed the button which would summon it from the depths of the tunnel system below and waited while it lumbered upward, emitting clanking and squealing sounds as if complaining about having to make the trip. I entered and pushed the button for "down." As I descended I watched walls of blue-gray clay rolling by. When the elevator reached the tunnel floor and stopped with a thud, I got my first glimpse of the subterranean railway.

The tunnel itself was an egg shaped arch with a flat floor along which rails were embedded. Overhead wires supplied the electricity to run the trains. The walls were coated with a kind of stucco, for water proofing I supposed. It didn't seem at all damp or musty. In fact, air circulation was quite adequate. I was at a kind of grand junction where three tunnels came together and the visual effect was not unlike that of a miniature cathedral.

I could hear the echoing of an approaching train as I stood on the slender platform that was Field's loading dock. The engine was about the size of a large automobile and it pulled a long line of freight cars filled with merchandise. Where Peter Dunning might have gone within this elaborate underground enterprise was a mystery. Had he "hopped" a train? Was he slithering along the narrow tunnel walls? There was no way to know. I returned to the basement above and made my way up the stairs into the building proper.

I wandered through the main floor amid glass counters filled with perfumes and lip gloss. I found the cosmetics section patently uninteresting and gravitated toward men's wallets and gloves. This soon became boring and my gaze traveled upward along decorated pillars toward the high ceiling where Tiffany mosaic glass glistened in the noon-day sunlight. Wonderful. I found the elevator and took it to the sixth floor so I could get a closer look at the dome.

Someone once told me there were one million, six-hundred thousand individual pieces of colored glass used in its construction. It was a masterpiece of geometric design, not unlike photographs I'd seen of the Arabic mosaics inside the medina of Fes in Morocco. Large stained-glass globes hung at either end of the ceiling, illuminating the iridescent favrile glass.

Each floor bordering the atrium allowed the shopper to peer over a railing to view the dome, or the floor below, or to watch people on other floors across the wide space. I looked down to marvel at the sight of glass-topped counters and aisles filled with woman wearing large, feathered hats, so small and insignificant; as if I were gazing through the roof of a doll's house. They hurried and scurried hither and there, no doubt as entranced by the opulent merchandise as I was by their insect-like activity. A clock on the wall told me it was almost noon. I had to hurry to make my appointment with Alicia Kaminski.

Instead of the elevator, I rode down the moving staircase, which is called an escalator, I believe. It was much faster than waiting for the elevator, but a bit tedious as it necessitated rounding a corner at each floor to seek out the next flight of moving stairs. I took this to the second floor mezzanine and found the employee cafeteria at one end of the floor behind a gift wrapping station. As I entered, my eye was caught by a sign which read:

NOTICE: *It is the wish and purpose of the house that no employee, no matter how unimportant his or her position may be, shall be forgotten or lost sight of; but instead, that every one whose name is on the payroll shall be recognized as a part of this great force, and that his or her efforts shall be carefully and frequently considered by the one above them in authority.*

Such was the inspirational message from the "House of Field." Next to it was another, smaller sign which read, "Today's Special: Mrs. Herring's Chicken Pot Pie." I sat at an empty table in the corner and started thinking about that pie when Alicia entered the room. I had seen Alicia Kaminski's pale blue eyes before, on the face of her mother. Alicia's did not have that mournful, dejected look, however. Instead, they radiated a jubilance that was intoxicating. She had not yet been beaten down by life's unfairness, it seemed, and she suffused a lighthearted attitude which enchanted me. Enchanted though I might be, I needed more information about Peter Dunning and thought Alicia could provide it.

"How long have you and Peter Dunning been together?" I asked once the girl had sat down.

"Together? What do you mean?"

"You know, romantically." This brought about a resounding laugh that turned heads at nearby tables.

"Peter and I aren't...romantic!" she exclaimed. "Peter is with Sammy."

"Sammy...that would be Samantha?"

"No, no. Samuel. My brother, Samuel and Peter are...are..."

"Together? Romantically? You mean they are..."

"Yes. You didn't know that? That's how I know Peter."

It seemed extraordinary...not just that the two men were...as they were, but because they came from such different social strata. I have always considered myself a good listener and I put this talent to work, coaxing more details from Alicia.

"He started coming round the house," Alicia told me. "Sammy and I are pretty close. We talk about everything, you know. He told me he and Peter loved each other. At first I was shocked, but then, when I saw how happy he made Sammy, I was glad for him."

She said she didn't know *everything* about her brother and Peter Dunning—or, perhaps, she declined to admit that certain irregularities of behavior may have...must have occurred, but I was able to glean a fair accounting of their sordid history.

There was a club where they had met. Somewhere on the Near South Side, she indicated. This I assumed must have been in the Levee District, and from my own somewhat shameful knowledge of the area, I thought I knew which one. At first I thought of The Everleigh Club. But it was much too fancy of a venue for the boys. It could be attended by referral only, had elaborate furnishings including a gold-leafed grand piano, elegant meals, and cost $50 a night. I wasn't aware that it featured entertainment by anything other than girls, although in the Levee, anything was possible. The rumor was that Marshall Field Jr, the only son of Alicia's employer, had been fatally shot by one of the prostitutes at the Everleigh Club. I wondered if Alicia knew that story.

There were plenty of other possibilities: Bed Bug Row, the California, Vic Shaw's, The Bucket of Blood or Black May's, but my money was on The Why Not. This was a pretty despicable institution with blacked-out windows in which fairly extreme perversities were said to be the main attraction. I was certain homosexuality was probably one of these. I didn't believe sweet and innocent Alicia, no matter how intimate she and her brother's heart-to-heart conversations had been, had any idea of the scope of the depravity represented by just about any of the establishments in the Levee. I was pleased that there was a concerted effort underway to shut down the many palaces of ill-repute in that 4-square block area—this in spite of political payoffs and the patronage (at least at the Everleigh) by public officials, wealthy and influential businessmen and the like.

So here were two young men from different walks of life, met and befriended in an unthinkably sleazy atmosphere, bonded in a common understanding of the differences of their natures from that of the norm, and both confronting stern opposition from parents and peers. Of course they would opt to take themselves away from the inevitable conflicts, possible retributions and the shaming, shunning, and slander that would follow. I wondered if Connie knew the truth about her brother. I had to bet that her father did.

I sat silently, at a complete loss for words. I knew about such things, of course, but I had never personally known anyone who was so inclined...or had I? Now it appeared I had an acquaintance who danced to a different drummer. Well, it was a new century. To each his own, I figured.

"Peter's sister came to me," I explained, "because Peter had disappeared. We thought it was a woman—you, in fact. We were worried that the two of you had eloped or something. I've been trying to find Peter and bring him home. His father is concerned as well."

"His father! I've heard quite a bit about that old Scrooge. He threatened to cut Peter out of his will, he did. Won't give him any money."

It's funny how the mind works. Here I was, deeply involved in the trials and tribulations of my former girl friend's brother, and something Alicia had just alluded to clicked open a mental switch in my consciousness. I thought: "Cut him out of the will...of course! That's the motive for the murder in the locked room." I was disgusted with myself for straying so blatantly from the issue at hand, if only in my mind. And Alicia must have sensed my discomfort as her normally radiant smile became a dark frown.

"Perhaps we should get some food," I said. "I hear Mrs. Herring's Chicken Pot Pie is being featured today."

We went through the cafeteria line, pushing wooden trays along steel rails, each selecting a bit of fruit, coffee and a glorious looking bowl topped with flaky pie crust, beneath which the promise of juicy lumps of chicken, succulent vegetables and potatoes lay steaming. I insisted on paying even though Alicia shook her head. We returned to the table and I dug into the pie with relish, but finding it too hot for the mouth, blew across my fork; this elicited a snicker from my companion.

"Sorry about my table manners," I said. It was nice to see the smile that broadened across that pretty face. Maybe some other time, some other place, this young woman and I...but no, I had business to attend to.

"Do you have any idea how I could locate Peter?" I asked.

"I'm sorry. I don't," she answered. "I haven't seen Sammy for a few days, either. Perhaps it will all work itself out." Not likely, I thought.

"It's funny, we know that Peter hates his father. Why would he go down into the tunnels when his father owns the rail company that runs there?" I said.

"I think when Sammy first started seeing Peter, Peter got him a part time job in the tunnels, working on one of the trains. It didn't last long. But I suppose it becomes natural to travel throughout the city that way, once you are used to it and you know the patterns. And if the two of them are together, it makes sense they would use the tunnels."

"Your own personal subway...and free at that! And a good place to hide. That's very helpful, Alicia. I know where to start looking...but, he could be anywhere in the city by now. Especially since he saw that I noticed him."

"You've got your job cut out for you. And I have mine, and I have to return to work now. If you see Sammy, tell him I'm on his side."

"Do your parents know?"

"Father doesn't. I think Mother suspects. She would never berate him for his behavior so long as it wasn't out in the open. Appearances, you know. But she loves him. Father, on the other hand…"

"Alicia, after this is all over, may I call on you?"

Her smile told me what her silence at my question had not. I walked her back to the loading area and we bid each other goodbye. I stood looking at the gate to the freight elevator, wondering if I had the wherewithal to descend again into the subterranean depths of the city, to search out the object of my quest. It was sort of pointless, I decided. I would have to report back to Connie now that I had come so close to encountering her brother that I had failed. And there was the issue of his homosexuality…I wasn't anxious to broach that subject with her. Would the couple return to their haunts in the Levee? I could check out The Why Not and the Bucket of Blood and some of the others.

I drove to South State Street and parked a few blocks from the Levee district, not wishing my automobile to be stolen or vandalized, and walked down toward the Everleigh Club. There were some famous old brothels here. Madam Emma Duvall's "French Em" had been here since the 1890's—it was said the walls and ceilings of her bedrooms were paneled with mirrors. The Lone Star Saloon was gone now. That notorious establishment had had a bartender by the name of Mickey Finn who would put knockout drops in the drinks in order to pick people's pockets. There were other areas in the city where gambling and prostitution had been raging for years: Gambler's Row, Whiskey Row, the Custom House…much of it had been destroyed in the Great Fire…but rose again like a phoenix in the area now known as the Levee.

The dives, called "resorts" by the cynical, were protected by payoffs to "Gray Wolf" aldermen like "Bathhouse" John Coughlin, "Hinky Dink" Mike Kenna, and Johnny Powers. It surprised me, therefore, that as I neared the Everleigh Club, I witnessed policemen (wearing those beehive hats that make them look like London Bobbies), ushering a group of scantily dressed young girls from the building and piling them into waiting police vans. There was a Chinese girl among them who I believed was the famous Suzy Poon Tang, and two older women who I knew to be the Everleigh sisters, Minna and Ada. It was a raid! I decided to reverse my direction and head back to the Jefferson League Club to confer with Rodney.

5

The Murder

It was late afternoon before I arrived back at the Jefferson League Club. I fell exhausted into an overstuffed chair in the alcove that Rodney and I favored. Bruce brought me a Scotch and I waited impatiently for Rodney to appear. Looking out the leaded glass window I could just see the white-tipped waves of Lake Michigan. It seemed a peaceful vista after my day of traveling throughout Chicago's stranger locales. I thought about the unlikelihood of ever finding Peter Dunning. I didn't relish the prospect of telling Connie about her brother's inclinations either. I was pondering this quandary when Rodney's bushy head bobbed into my line of sight.

"Hello, old sport," he said.

"Hello, yourself. I've been waiting for you."

"Oh? Something on your mind."

"Several things. I need your insights on a problem I've been involved in...concerning the brother of my friend, Constance Dunning. First, though, I have solved your 'locked room' mystery!"

"Ah, you have! Let's have it then."

"It was the son who killed him. The father was about to cut him out of his will. That's why he had shut himself into his study. But knowing that his father usually locked himself in, the son decided to administer a slow acting poison. The father succumbed to this while locked in his study, about to change the will, and slumped over the desk. The maid summoned the son, who broke down the door. All the maid saw was the father with his head on the desk. The son sent her away just long enough to shoot the father in the head with a bullet from his rifle which was disguised as a walking stick. Hence the slowly leaking pool of blood. When the policeman arrived he assumed the murder was committed with a gun, which could not be found. That's it!"

"Ah, no. That isn't it," said Rodney. I was crushed. My brilliant deduction was apparently way off base. I was stymied once again. I proceeded to bring Rodney up to date about the Peter Dunning affair, if I may be permitted to use that word to describe it. He listened thoughtfully but ventured no recommendation on what action I should take, if any, at this point. I sincerely wanted his input and advice as I respected his intellect and moral judgment.

"I am most concerned," I said, "with Connie's anxiety and insecurity. Peter Dunning, even though he is now living a life apart from the expectations of friends and family, can certainly take care of himself. I'm still a little confused as to exactly what the girl is afraid of."

"I would think," Rodney commented, "that therein lies the rub, so to speak. If you can determine the answer to that question, I think you will be far ahead in bringing things to a satisfactory conclusion. Perhaps it would be prudent to question this girl further...talk to her without seeming to question, that is. She sounds to me to be on the defensive. Do you really think she is unaware of her brother's proclivities?"

"Why wouldn't she have told me? She'd have to realize I would find out eventually."

"Maybe she is underestimating you."

We sat, meditating, drinks and cigars the only tools at our disposal when Bruce burst upon us with a worried look on his face and handed me a note. It was from Connie:

Come quickly! Father has been murdered!

It seemed this dreadful news carried with it the answer to our question: what was Connie afraid of? Rodney would have instructed me, had I asked for his opinion at that particular time, not to assume that Peter Dunning had murdered his father. To wait for the facts. But I couldn't shake the feeling that this was inexorably true. It explained Connie's concern for Peter's whereabouts, her admonition to me *not* to bring him home as her father had insisted—and there was that cryptic note Connie had shown me in which Peter said, "*Father makes me so angry sometimes that I wish he were dead!*" And Peter had added: "*I must do what I must do.*"

I enlisted Rodney's aid by literally dragging him from his chair and ushering him downstairs. We collected our outdoor gear and tumbled into the Overland. I spared none of the horses, so to speak, in whisking us up to the Dunning mansion on Wrightwood. On the way I complained to Rodney that he really hadn't given me many clues to the locked room puzzle. To this he replied, "Well, you didn't ask the right questions, old man."

I parked around the corner, taking note of the police wagon out front. The door was ajar so we entered, unannounced, and followed the faint sound of voices coming from the study off the second floor landing. Up the marble staircase we went, taking the steps two at a time. Upon entering the room I saw a policeman in uniform and a man in a plain brown suit standing over two very distraught women who I recognized as Connie and her mother. The plain clothes man turned and said, in a curt baritone, "And who might you be?"

I knew that Chicago police detectives were selected, not from the smartest, most capable candidates, but from those with the most political influence. I had little confidence in this man, or in any of the police for that matter, regarding their willingness to apprehend criminals, much less their ability to do so—unless, of course, there was a sizable profit in the offing. I know this view of our local constabulary, their corruption and laziness, may seem harsh, but it was the status quo in those days. Even their half-hearted attempts to close down the Levee district with its gambling and cat houses were riddled with stories of graft and malfeasance. I was positive that the raid I had seen earlier would result in more profits for the police department and an appalling lack of jurisprudence for the curtailing of vice. Consequently, I didn't proffer any explanation for our presence but turned toward Connie with an expression of deep concern.

Connie made the informal introductions that seemed necessary and told the plain clothes detective, whose name and rank were

Detective Lieutenant Andrew Clancy, that we were good friends of the family and that she had requested our assistance. He scoffed and inquired, "And what would you be knowin' about this business?"

Rodney rose to the occasion with a response that seemed to placate the detective and indulge his authoritarianism without much oblique mollycoddling:

"We are here," he said, "to offer any assistance we can to you in your investigation. We know what fine work the police have done in uncovering criminal activities and we also know how thinly spread they are these days what with the moral degradation that plagues our fine city. We hope we can provide an additional perspective on this tragedy, so we are at your service."

"Well," said Detective Lieutenant Andrew Clancy, "this kind lady of the house, Mrs. Dunning, has told me what transpired only a few hours previous. I guess it is all right if I let you in on the details. It appears her husband, Mr. Dunning, was here in this room with some visitors of whose identities we are uncertain at this point."

"There was more than one?"

"She feels from the different range of the voices she heard that there were two men in with her husband. Their voices were loud, like in an argument, she says, but too muffled to be understood. This lasted for some minutes while Mrs. Dunning went to the kitchen to talk to the cook, isn't that right, Ma'am?"

The effect of being questioned again by this crude man sent Mrs. Irene Dunning into spasms of sobbing. Connie embraced her with a protective hug and the sobbing began to subside. Mrs. Dunning nodded in the affirmative.

"Well anyway, as Mrs. Dunning was climbing the stairs to inform her husband as to the dining arrangements, she heard a loud thud as if a body had fallen to the floor." (Here, Mrs. Dunning gasped and began again to sob.) "So she opened the door and found him here, next to the desk."

The body had by this time been removed but a dark stain on the carpet indicated where he had lain. There was a small cast-bronze statue, a miniature replica of Rodin's "The Thinker," lying on its side near what I assumed was dried blood. Rodney immediately began examining the carpet and the area around the desk. I was about to ask about the two visitors when Detective Clancy said, "Except for the body, the room was empty!"

I thought of Peter Dunning and his friend, Samuel Kaminski. Could they have been the two voices Mrs. Dunning had overheard? A glance at Connie told me she had read my thoughts. She flashed me a warning with a subtle shake of her head and the mouthed words, "Please, don't." I remained mute. By this time, Mrs. Dunning was crying uncontrollably. Connie led her away from the bloody room and the insensitive policeman. "What will you do next?" I asked Detective Lieutenant Andrew Clancy.

"Oh, we'll have a dragnet, of course. Round up all the likely suspects. We'll find 'em. The beat cops know all the local boys and their rackets. These guys must have panicked and took off before they could steal anything."

"Mrs. Dunning saw them leave?"

"Ah, no. But they must of got by her somehow. No other way out of here."

Rodney beckoned me with a nod. "Well, good luck, Lieutenant," he offered. "We must be on our way." I found myself swept down the staircase and out into the street before I could extract the slightest comment from my friend. Once we had climbed into the Overland and I had the motor rumbling, Rodney exclaimed, "To Marshall Field's!"

"You're thinking, as I am, that it was Peter and his friend?" I queried as we flew down the Drive at a breakneck speed."

"That is a possibility. And, oh that policeman is an imbecile! All he had to do was to look at the carpet to understand what happened. The cops in this town are worthless! All they can do is arrest vagrants and shake down confidence men. Worthless!"

"What about the carpet?"

"There were tracks on the carpet that led around behind the desk and then stopped."

"And that means?"

"It means there was another exit from the room. Probably hidden behind a bookcase. A swinging door disguised as a bookcase would be my guess. It also suggests that the killer or killers were familiar with it."

"Why didn't Mrs. Dunning or Connie mention that to the detective?"

"Because, obviously, he didn't ask the right questions."

We parked on State Street and entered Field's. "Show me this elevator," Rodney said. I took him there and soon we were descending into the crepuscular caverns below. If elves or dwarves had appeared I would not have been surprised. We stood on the platform as a train pulled up, its cars filled with ash. Rodney hailed the engineer and quizzed him: did he know a Samuel Kaminski or a Peter Dunning?

"No, can't say's I do. But if I were lookin' for somebody, I'd try the Jackson Street Station. There's lockers there and a body kin take his breaks in the break room."

"How do we find the Jackson Street Station?"

"Go down three intersections and turn right. Another four and you're there. Hop on and I'll take you part ways."

We rode the electric engine for a few blocks then went the remainder of the distance on foot, keeping well toward the walls as the space was narrow and a rampaging train could appear at any given time. We reached the station, an underground hamlet for the hundreds of tunnel workers. There was a hodgepodge of smells in the place: the hot odor of electrified air, the aroma of stifling dust and dirt that swirled off passing trains and clung to the nostrils with an oily tang, the sweet, acrid smell of discarded fruit and half-eaten sandwiches thrown into an ash can, the sweat of a myriad of men in close quarters and the faint memory of once fresh air pushed through the tunnels by the trains.

We sat on wooden chairs. What ever could we do to locate the two fugitives, if indeed that was what they were? What would we do once we found them? We were not officials of the police. We had no weapons should the encounter become contentious. In fact, we had no proof they had committed the crime or had been present at the scene. I voiced these doubts to Rodney in hopes he had some knowledge I hadn't.

"I felt an urgency," he replied, "to eliminate one possible solution to the murder. I felt that if we could question the son, we could get closer to the truth."

"I don't understand. Didn't Peter kill his father?"

"That is speculation at this point. Finding him in these tunnels is like finding a needle in a haystack. Every street in the loop has one running under it. Besides, the tunnels link up with several railroads. They could grab a ride on the Great Western or the Santa Fe and be out of the state in a flash!"

As we sat there, the walls and the low ceiling of the break room seemed to press in on me. I'm not that prone to claustrophobia but this chamber within the labyrinth of endless burrows was testing my metal. It was dismal and dreary down there and the uncertainty of the situation tormented me. After what seemed like hours but surely was only minutes, I felt Rodney grasp me by the arm. "Quiet," he whispered, although I had said nothing. Then I saw the reason for his cautioning gesture. Two men had appeared in the space and had gone swiftly to a locker along the far wall. One of them was Peter Dunning.

They retrieved a gray ruck sack from the locker. Rodney leaped toward the pair; I followed. Peter turned and recognized me at once. Then pandemonium ensued as Peter and Samuel scrambled to evade us. Down the tunnel they ran with Rodney and myself in close pursuit. But the years and soft lounging at the Jefferson League Club had us soon huffing and puffing and losing ground in the race.

At each tunnel crossing we had to pause and listen to be sure of the direction they had taken. They were eluding us, that was certain. There were no air shafts leading to the surface as the city hadn't allowed manholes when the tunnels were built. The only exit up was through various connections to commercial buildings or freight terminals. Samuel Kaminski certainly knew where these escape hatches would be. We didn't.

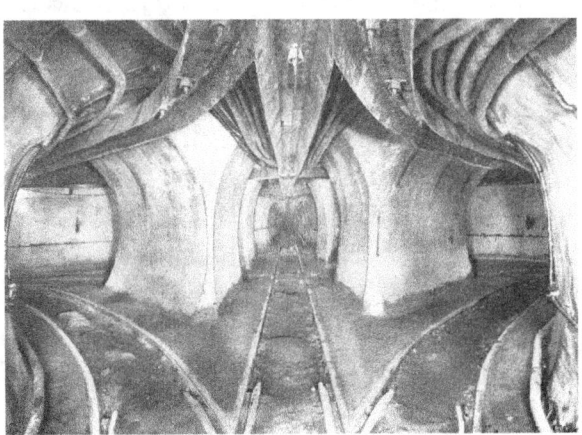

We came to an intersection where three tunnels came together. Again I was reminded of a European cathedral or the catacombs beneath it. Were there ancient, crumbling coffins with the remains of the Knights Templar buried within these walls? Underground like that, with no glimpse of sun or clue as to direction, my mind was playing tricks. I could feel rats running up my legs, although no such rodents were in evidence.

We were uncertain as to which tunnel to take; the sounds of footfalls had diminished to the point that only faint echoes could be heard without indicating their origin. Then, all at once, we heard another sound. A train was coming toward us at high speed! The overhead lights began to blink and flicker and suddenly were extinguished. A great piercingly bright light swung around a bend in one of the tunnels ahead of us. It was coming down the left turning so we leaped into the darkness where we thought the right turning was, blinded by the rushing headlamp and guided only by sheer luck.

The train passed. We sat, panting, on the ties in the adjoining tunnel. After a few moments, the lights flickered back on. We were stymied; we had been literally in the dark during this ill-fated chase. Should we continue? In which direction? At what risk to life and limb? At last we relented, returning as best we could to the Jackson Street Station where an elevator took us to the street level. I gulped the fresh air hungrily. We walked back in defeated silence to my automobile.

"Now what?" I asked.

"Ducktown is our only option," replied Rodney, his usual self-assured demeanor slacking into a desperate glower. I understood. Samuel would want to see his mother one last time before the grand exodus to parts unknown. I was still dubious that we would achieve anything by accosting the pair, but Rodney's tenacity eclipsed my skepticism and disquietude. Off we would go to the land of muck and mud with all hope of keeping my roadster shiny a lost cause.

"You aren't convinced that Peter killed his father?"

"He and Samuel were certainly there. The footprints prove that. But..."

"But?"

"There were three sets of prints. One considerably smaller than the others."

I considered this statement and what it implied. A woman. The mother was outside the room. So that meant...

"You mean...Connie!"

"Did you notice what she was wearing when we saw her today?"

"It was something beige, I think. A frock."

"The shoes?"

"I didn't notice the shoes."

"They were blue. Powder blue pumps."

"So, what does that prove?"

"She is an immaculate dresser. She would never wear those shoes with that dress. Clearly, she changed them before the police came. Also, consider the murder weapon: a small statue."

"The Thinker, yes. Oh, I see. You think of that as a woman's style of weapon?"

"It was a weapon of convenience. The murder wasn't planned. It was passionate. Maybe even self defense or an act of protection."

"The raised voices. Peter is arguing with his father. Connie enters. Peter and his father struggle. Connie picks up the statue, and…"

"We don't know that for sure. I need to talk to Peter."

We climbed into the Overland and I set off for the Kaminski household in Ducktown. It was not a confrontation I was looking forward to. Would we even find Samuel of Peter there? I had to doubt it. The prospect of seeing Alicia Kaminski again was the only positive aspect of this venture…although I dearly wished it could be under better circumstances.

Byron Grush

6

A Pronouncement of Sorts

Dusk was deepening into a dark purplish miasma you could cut with a knife. As we arrived at the house the only illumination in this starless gloom was a tint of gold to the southwest, the result, I surmised, of gases from the Bubbly Creek bursting into flames as was commonplace. An eerie silence completed the abysmal emptiness of Mount Pleasant. We two strangers in this strange land climbed the rickety steps to the porch and I banged on the dilapidated door for a second time that day. It was opened by Alicia Kaminski.

"It's you, is it?" she said fiercely. "And who is this with you? More of Williard Dunning's private army?"

"Alicia," I pleaded, "I don't know what you mean. This is Rodney Morton…he's a friend. I need to talk to Sammy, Alicia. He may be in trouble."

"He and Peter were here earlier this afternoon. They're going away. They won't be back. Somehow, this is your fault, isn't it?"

"No, no, I…"

"He wouldn't be leaving except for that ogre of a father of Peter's. And you've been sent to chase after him."

"You don't know?"

"I don't know what?"

"Peter's father is dead. He was killed today." I could see by the look on Alicia Kaminski's face that she didn't know Dunning was dead. So either Sammy and Peter had been here before the murder, or they had elected not to tell her…or maybe they hadn't been present when Dunning was killed at all!

"What? And you think…oh, no! Not Sammy. Not Peter. They could never…"

"We only want to talk with them. See if we can get to the bottom of this horrible thing."

"And then do what? Arrest them? Send them to prison? To the gallows? Please go away! I don't want to talk to you or see you ever again!" She slammed the door in my face.

I backed sheepishly down the stairs. Rodney, frowning, followed me back to the Overland. We drove away with no particular destination in mind this time as it seemed we were at an end. A very dead end. There was one person I didn't want to see and that was Connie. I couldn't bear to think she might be responsible for her father's death, even if she *was* protecting her brother. The prospect that Peter had killed him in a rage over his father's rejection of his lover, although despicable, was preferable to me. If the killer had to be a family member—which we were fairly certain was the truth of the matter—my money was on Peter.

I'd started the day with two women in my life: one from a former romance that could, none the less, blossom back into full bloom, and another, potentially a new romance, a fair flower that needed nurturing. And now I had neither. I was despondent. I dropped Rodney off at the Jefferson League Club and drove to my house, the house, that is, that had belonged to my parents. I was tired and the prospect of spending the evening at the club with Rodney, hashing over all that had happened, appealed to me very little.

Just as he was about to exit the roadster I assailed Rodney with yet another theory of the locked room mystery. His explanation that the murderer or murderers had left through a hidden doorway at the Dunning's promoted a similar notion in my approach to that other murder, the fictional one Rodney had proposed. And so I postulated that there was, indeed, a secret panel in the locked room. Rodney replied, "Sorry, old man. No secret panel. You'll have to do better than that." I drove home, totally defeated on all fronts.

My house on North Astor Street was modest by comparison to many of the elaborate Gold Coast mansions: Palmer's castle, of course, Robert Todd Lincoln's huge estate, the luxurious abodes of the likes of playwright Kenneth Sawyer Goodman, liquor magnate Albert F. Madlener, timber baron James Charnley, steel and iron industrialist Joseph T. Ryerson Jr., and Archbishop Patrick Feehan. My humble home was a mere 5,000 square feet, four stories and had only 5 bedrooms. The terracotta-colored brick work set it off nicely from others on the elm-lined street. It had rounded, turret-like rooms on two different levels where I loved to sit.

Astor Street, named for John Jacob Astor (who never lived in Chicago, by the way), was dotted with domiciles of the very wealthy from North Avenue to Bishop's Street. Much of the property had been developed by Potter Palmer, and my father had been involved in several of the real estate deals. This was the stamping grounds for protagonists of the Gilded Age, as Mark Twin called it. Here had been a gathering of the tribes who had built up the economy of the elite on the blood and sweat of the working classes. Here was the home I had inherited, but where I rarely stayed, preferring life at the club and its proximity to the Loop where I could walk to museums and concert halls and restaurants.

I keep a minimal staff to run the house. There was an elderly couple, George and Hilda Mandel, who were my butler and cook, respectively, and Minnie Kovacs, a matronly woman who was drab and sometimes cranky, but who kept the place tidy in her capacity as maid. I was exorbitantly fatigued, but also famished. I rang for George and asked him to have Mrs. Mandel put together some cold meat and cheese for me and a glass of cold milk.

I settled into the easy chair in my second floor reading room. Dear Mrs. Mandel brought my snack along with two slices of freshly baked rye and a small jar of mustard. I had intended to forego any thoughts of murders or locked rooms, but my mind wandered into those realms like a small boy lost in a forest, forgetting to drop a trail of bread crumbs to find his way back. Soon I was in a half-dream state, with trap doors and sliding bookcases and weapons disguised as everything from umbrella handles to door stops.

My eyelids drooped and a haze seemed to form in front of me. I shook this off and found my refocused vision tracing a line across the bookshelf as if searching for some microscopic nit of inspiration. There sat a copy of the works of Poe. His "Murders in the Rue Morgue" was the story of a young woman found strangled and mutilated, and stuffed up the chimney in a *locked room*. Here the solution of the crime revealed an escaped orangutan, the animal leaving by the window and climbing to the rooftop.

Next the red leather bindings of my collection of Conan Doyle's Sherlock Holms stories entered my field of vision. In "The Adventure of the Speckled Band" Holmes is confronted by a seemingly impossible murder in a locked room. The solution? A poisonous snake crawling down the bell cord. Another murder by an animal. Neither of these stories aided me in my obsession with Rodney's mystery or the murder of Willard Dunning. What else might my library offer in the way of analysis?

A young woman has been assaulted. She locks herself in her bedroom, but falls from the bed hitting her head on the bedside table, resulting in partial amnesia. It appears she has been the victim of an invisible attacker when she is found in the room (which is still locked from inside) and can remember nothing. This was part of the plot of a favorite story of mine, Gaston Leroux's "The Mystery of the Yellow Room." But I had suggested something of this kind to Rodney—the man was shot elsewhere and locked himself in the room before he died. I was rebuked; why was there no trail of blood? No, this story was also of no help to me.

Well, I believe it was Lord Byron who said truth is stranger than fiction. And somehow I was mixing up the fictional and the real life murders in my befuddled mind. I fell asleep in my chair that night, the half-eaten sandwich testifying to my utter exhaustion…both physical and mental. I dreamed of orangutans and rushing subway trains…and the angelic faces of two young women.

Minnie was shaking me. "You've gone and slept in your chair," she scolded. "Rise and shine…it's nearly noon! What do you want for breakfast?"

I rubbed my eyes. "Just tell Mrs. Mandel to brew me a pot of her eggshell coffee. That's all I can handle today."

"Nonsense! You'll get a stack of griddle cakes and some fresh grilled kielbasa. What have we got a stock yards for if a body can't have good Chicago sausage to stick to his bones?"

She had dumped a stack of unopened correspondence and the morning newspaper on my lap. I pushed aside the letters and picked up the Times. The headline said: "Great Drama at Republican

Convention." Ordinarily, politics bore me to tears. I hadn't been following the presidential primaries for either party. But here was a story that promised some distraction. I read.

Former president Theodore Roosevelt and his supporters had stormed out of the Chicago Coliseum last night when it became clear that incumbent President William Howard Taft had tied up the votes of at least 248 delegates—although Roosevelt had won nearly all the preferential primaries. Taft was trying to steal the nomination! It had been, so far, a convention of cat calls and booing. Four years ago, Roosevelt, obeying the unwritten tradition that no American president ever ran for more than two terms, had hand-picked Taft as his successor. Taft had proven to be a turncoat, abandoning Roosevelt's progressive policies. This so infuriated Teddy that he now ran for a third term. The party establishment, under Taft's leadership, wasn't having any of Roosevelt's bluster, and ignored the primary results in order to oust Roosevelt.

Roosevelt had reconvened his own supporters at Chicago's Orchestra Hall in a split from the Republican Party and so a new party, the Progressive Party, had been born. The reporter commented that it was likely that the Republicans and the Progressives would have to divide the votes of their base in the upcoming election, giving the Democratic candidate, a somewhat unknown man named Woodrow Wilson, a leg up and a possible win. We would just have to see what would happen in November, I thought. Well, what would it matter to me?

You may think me callous and insensitive for my apathy toward the political process, but I deemed it preposterous that the ordinary man on the street could have any affect on the direction of our so-called democracy. A handful of rich and powerful people pulled the strings—I was not among them, being not wealthy enough to have influence, and certainly disinterested—but not totally heartless—in matters where government intersected with everyday life. Perhaps once women got the vote things would change.

Weeks passed. There was no news of Peter and Samuel. The newspapers reported that Detective Lieutenant Andrew Clancy had arrested Willard Dunning's killer, a vagrant who had been seen in the neighborhood. This was good news...or was it? I remembered Rodney's characterization of Detective Clancy as a buffoon who had missed all the important clues. Had the police simply gone out and picked someone at random so that they could put the case to rest? It seemed likely.

I hadn't seen Connie since the day of the murder. An intense yearning overtook me and I surrendered my common sense to the lovelorn urges of my solitude. I sent a note: would she see me? A note returned: please come.

She answered the door herself when I arrived at the Dunning Manson. She was even lovelier than I remembered. Her face, though, showed signs of former stress: little creases that barely disappeared as she smiled at me. I hoped my reaction to her obvious distress wasn't apparent. I took both of her hands in mine.

"Connie, I'm so sorry I haven't rung you up before this. I know you've been grieving and I should have been here for you. But I... "

"I know. I know what you think and I can't blame you. Father was...he could be terrible. A tyrant. He treated Peter like a slave and an ingrate. Peter actually worshipped him, you know. I was so sad when he..."

"You don't have to tell me about it."

She led me into the sitting room. We sat on a green velvet divan behind which a giant fern spread delicate fronds. It could almost have been a pleasant tête-à-tête between two old friends or a sensual rendezvous between two lovers...but it was neither. It was an encounter in which avoidance could be vanquished only through unabashed honesty and trust. Did I have her trust?

"Connie, you can trust me...tell me anything. Peter is out of it now. That fool policeman has arrested some poor tramp for the crime. They won't be able to convict him for there is no evidence, but it means they are not looking at anyone in the family..."

"You think Peter murdered my father, don't you."

"I...I don't know, but it does seem like the logical conclusion. He did run."

Of course, in the back of my mind, the notion that Connie was also a suspect returned to vex me. This must have shown on my countenance as a thinly masked denunciation. Connie held my furtive glance with sad eyes. Silence and frozen looks followed for what seemed like an eternity...I was so close to the truth, but repelled by its consequences. We tried talking of trivialities. Connie suggested tea...why tea, I thought? I could have downed a tumbler of Scotch with little effort. But eventually, both of us knew we would need to return to the subject we were evading.

I started to broach the subject with small hints as to Rodney's theory of the crime, but still could not bring myself to accuse Connie. Then, coolly, without tears or trembling, this woman I believed I loved, told me the following:

"That day, Peter and Sammy came to see father, to try to make him understand, to accept them as partners. Of course Father was livid. I can't repeat the horrible oaths that poured from his mouth. It was like seeing a beloved and saintly man transformed into a raging devil! His very body seemed to be on fire like a torch and words leaped out like flames at poor Peter and Sammy. Father stormed from the room and shut himself in his study.

"Mother and I, having witnessed the tirade, tried to commiserate and calm the men, but it became apparent they could not let things stand as they were. Up the stairs they went...and we feared the worse for the outcome. Mother was trembling. I went to the kitchen to get her a glass of water. I hoped beyond hope that Father would have settled down, that Peter would be approaching him in a civilized manner. But it was not to be.

"They three were in the study. They continued arguing. You could hear them all over the house. Mother and I were still downstairs, giving each other uneasy looks. She told me she had to do something about the ugly confrontation. She had to intercede, break up the fight. I told her to stay where she was. She wouldn't listen to me. She'd always been a mild-mannered woman who had let Father trample all over her ego. But this pushed her over the edge. I saw a light flare up behind her eyes that I'd never seen before. She went upstairs to the room where they were."

I sat listening to Connie unravel her tale with trepidation. She would soon come to the time of the murder and I would learn the truth. I wanted to stop her right there...I should have. Should have taken her in my arms and kissed her and chased the guilt away with a show of unconditional regard. But I let her continue.

"I heard a scream. I hurried up the stairs and saw Father on the floor in a pool of blood. The statue was in my mother's hands. Peter and Sammy stood agape and motionless. It was if the scene were frozen in time...and irrevocable. Oh...the blood...the blood!

"I told Peter and Sammy to leave by the hidden doorway which leads down some stairs and to the outside at the back of the house so they wouldn't be seen. Because I knew, I felt, that they would be blamed. I think now that in the back of my mind I *hoped* they would be blamed...so Mother wouldn't be suspected. I got Mother away from the study, got her cleaned up. We both changed clothes. I don't know how I was so cool. I was frightened, but I had to protect her and Peter. We came up with a story and called the police. The police came. Then you came. I knew you thought of Peter right away. I'm glad you said nothing. I'm glad you stayed away until now because I couldn't have faced you yet. But now I have."

Now I did take her in my arms, kissed her face. She pulled away from me. Before either of us could say anything, Helen, the maid entered and said to Connie: "Miss, excuse me, but that policeman is here at the door wanting to speak to you." This was an ironic bit of coincidence, I thought. Connie told the maid to show him in.

Detective Lieutenant Andrew Clancy marched proudly into the sitting room. I did not stand up. He had that arrogant look of the underclass when they are thrust into the presence of their betters and they project an illogical semblance of equality. I am, perhaps, being snobbish, but this ignorant flatfoot infuriated me. I shared Rodney's distain for the man and, now that I indeed knew the truth of the matter, I also feared him. What if Connie or I made a slip?

"Sorry to be disturbin' you, Miss," Clancy began. "You may have read in the papers about the capture, but I wanted to tell you in person. We have apprehended the dastard that murdered your father. It was police work at its best, if I do say so myself."

"That's...that's wonderful, Detective. You're sure you've got the right man?" asked Connie. I didn't want to pursue this line of inquiry, although I was curious how they had convinced themselves of this man's guilt in the face of no evidence whatsoever. I echoed her query.

"Yes, Detective, how can you be sure?" I blurted. I was instantly sorry I had said anything. It wouldn't do to have the police revisiting the case.

"We found the rascal sleeping in the park near where the old cemetery used to be. We pulled him in along with several other vagrants, but somehow he stood out as the likely candidate." (Notice Clancy here used the word "candidate" as if it were a contest for the title of society killer most excellent!) "We questioned him," Clancy continued, "with the usual means at hand and obtained a confession forthwith."

"A confession! Good work. Seems you *do* have the culprit." I was later to feel remorse at my jubilation for what was certainly an example of police brutality...the old "first degree" with a rubber hose, but I wasn't thinking at the time of the poor lout that would be languishing in a rat-infested jail for the rest of his life.

"I also need to inform you, Miss, that it will require yourself and your mother to testify in court as to what you saw and heard on that terrible day. We know it is a dreadful business to be so prolonged, but a conviction is essential. We'll hang the man...that is for sure!"

Byron Grush

7

The Trial

The trial began on October 14, a Monday, the same day that former president Theodore Roosevelt was shot. Teddy had been campaigning in Milwaukee and was greeting supporters in front of the Gilpatrick Hotel when a saloon keeper named John Schrank approached and fired with a .32-caliber hand gun, aiming directly at Roosevelt's heart. Roosevelt wore a heavy coat and in a breast pocket carried a case for his glasses and the thick manuscript of the speech he was to deliver. These slowed the bullet enough that it did not reach the vital organ, but he was still seriously wounded. Undaunted, Roosevelt insisted on speaking and stood for over 90 minutes, eventually pulling the bloody manuscript from his pocket and waving it triumphantly. "It takes more than one bullet to kill a Bull Moose," he yelled.

Connie and her mother were to report to the Cook County Criminal Court Building at 54 West Hubbard Street by 9:00 AM that morning. I had decided to accompany them for support, and frankly, out of curiosity about the prosecution of this drifter. Surely the case against him was circumstantial and so flimsy that he would be acquitted, perhaps even before Connie and her mother were to testify.

The first courthouse had been destroyed in the Great Fire, like

57

so many other buildings, both public and private. A new building, the second of three, was erected at the Hubard Street site. In 1875, Mary Todd Lincoln was put on trial there and declared insane by a jury who deliberated for all of 10 minutes. In 1886, the Haymarket Square Riot Trial took place in that same courthouse. Four union leaders were subsequently hanged.

True to the spirit of urban renewal in Chicago, which leaves no landmark untouched, the Courthouse was torn down in 1892 and replaced with this current Richardsonian building which featured a Romanesque style of architecture. It had great arched windows on the first story and a pillared balustrade on the second level over the entrance. Each of the three levels had a different treatment in terms of ornament and the roof was topped with a façade reminiscent of the Parthenon. Somehow this conglomeration all worked, presenting a solid, authoritarian edifice where justice was taken seriously. At least that was the assumption.

The Hubbard Street jail was located just in back of this and included a Murderers' Row and the hanging gallows...thus the complex was a one stop location for murderers and anarchists. Another notorious trial had taken place at the Courthouse in 1897 when Adolph Luetgert, known as the Sausage King of the North Side, was convicted of murdering his wife; he had placed his wife's body in his sausage making machine. Luetgert had spent nearly two years locked in an 8 by 8 foot cell in that jail while his trial took place.

The courtroom itself was as gloomy as the notion that condemned prisoners, now waiting on Death Row in the nearby jailhouse, had passed through here on their way to eternity and left behind a bit of their auras of doom. Everywhere was dark-stained paneling. There were no windows, only ceiling-mounted electric lights to provide illumination. The judge's bench was on a raised platform and the spectator area was separated from the court by a Baroque-looking railing. There was a painted mural on one wall of "The Wisdom of Solomon" depicting the ancient king upon his throne ordering a soldier to draw his sword and cut a child, the object of a dispute between two frantic women, into equal parts. This was going to prove to be an interesting setting for the trial.

Judge Herman James Hoffmeyer sat, berobed and bewhiskered, on his dais as majestic as King Solomon himself, and seemed ready to nod off as the bailiff administered the oath to the jury members. The jury, twelve *men* and true, seemed to be composed of white, middle-class clerks, salesmen, accountants, and only one or two who might be laborers. For the most part, these would not favor the defendant who would be portrayed as a "robber-murderer," the worst kind of cold-blooded killer. In fact, Assistant State's Attorney Leonard Houghton gave a scathing opening argument in which the unfortunate man was called a predator who would slink out into the night with malicious intent and wantonly take the life of peaceful citizens for the acquisition of a few mere trinkets.

I was beginning to have doubts about the ethical and logical acquittal of the vagrant. The man's name was Willy Borman who, it was told, was also known as "Slippery Willy." Evidence would be presented, the prosecutor told the jury, that the defendant had been arrested numerous times for petty larceny and vagrancy. Essential to the state's case was the confession, given freely, it was claimed; and the inherently evil character of the man which gave no doubt as to his capacity for this villainous assault *with intent to kill*. No motive was offered beyond that of discovery during a robbery.

It was time for the defense attorney to make his opening statement. A young man rose from the defense table. He looked to be just a boy of eighteen or possibly younger, although this was undoubtedly due to his slender build, sandy hair and freckled complication. What would the jury think of him? He had the unlikely name of Algernon Grimes, a slight stutter, and a very wrinkled, ill-fitting suit. Instead of rebutting the prosecution's characterization of his client, he simply said, in a barely audible voice, that the so-called confession had been coerced. He said that his client therefore retracted his confession and denied any knowledge of the alleged crime. The prosecution objected to the insinuation that the police were anything but honest and the judge agreed, instructing the jury to disregard Grimes' statement.

Now I knew we were in trouble. I say we, because by this time I was feeling real empathy for Slippery Willy and not a little guilt about my own knowledge of the real killer. There was nothing I could do, however. The public defender was incompetent or just inexperienced, there was most likely a presumption of guilt on the part of the jury...and there had been no alibi presented to place the defendant anywhere but at the scene of the crime. Added to that was the high profile aspect of the case, the victim being an important, wealthy, pillar of society, and (according to the prosecution), an frail, elderly man incapable of protecting himself against a raging lunatic like Slippery Willy.

Detective Lieutenant Andrew Clancy was called by the prosecution to describe the murder scene. He did this using explicit details of the amount of blood surrounding the body, the horrible grimace frozen on the dead man's face, the awkward tangle of limbs as if the body were a collapsed balloon. He told how the Lady of the house had discovered the body and how the daughter had contacted the department, how he and his men had hurried to the scene but, at that time, were unable to apprehend the fleeing assailant.

The fleeing assailant? Our astute public defender barely cross-examined the Lieutenant. He simply got the man to reiterate what he had already said. He was losing the opportunity to suggest an alternate version of the crime because no mention had been made of the voices Irene Dunning had heard arguing and that she had *reported* hearing to Detective Clancy. Surely Mrs. Dunning or Connie would offer this information during their testimony.

Assistant State's Attorney Leonard Houghton was skilled in the art of questioning witnesses to derive only the facts he considered pertinent to his case. Did Mrs. Dunning discover the body? Yes, she did. Did she send her daughter to contact the police? Yes, again. No further questions, your Honor. I suppose I shouldn't criticize Public Defender Algernon Grimes for failing to ask the right questions in his cross-examination; his client didn't know about the voices. He might have asked the Lady of the house to *tell in her own words* what had happened that night. He did not. A similar pattern occurred when Connie testified. She tried to interject just enough information into the record to establish a reasonable doubt but was admonished by Judge Hoffmeyer only to answer "yes" or "no" to the questions put to her by the prosecutor.

When Connie returned to her seat next to me in the audience section of the courtroom I whispered to her, "We have to get word to that defense attorney to suggest an alternate version of the crime. They are railroading this poor man."

"I can't let them suspect Mother," Connie replied. At that point I knew Slippery Willy was doomed.

Testimony was given as to the capture and questioning of the vagrant. Nothing was said about the third degree, nor was there any valid reason shown to suspect a homeless man, one of perhaps dozens of like unfortunates, who was not fleeing but was simply wrapped in a heavy coat against the cold and huddled under a bridge. The confession was read by the bailiff from a typed document that Borman had signed in a shaky hand. It was damning evidence.

In fact, the jury deliberated for under an hour, some of which was taken up by coffee breaks, no doubt. Slippery Willy Borman was found guilty of murder in the first degree. Judge Hoffmeyer stated he saw no reason to delay sentencing. Borman would be conducted to Murderers' Row in the County Jail where he would await execution...to be hung by the neck until dead!

I repaired to the Jefferson League Club to drown my despondency in a tall glass of 12 year-old scotch. I hadn't told Rodney everything I knew about the Dunning murder case before this, but it was evident that the old sleuth suspected that my despair was rooted in guilt and anger and knowledge unshared. After my second Scotch...this one without ice...I became a veritable flibbertigibbet blurting out all the facts and fancies of the legal farce I had just witnessed. At Rodney's prompting, the story that Connie had told me, that her mother was the murderer, was added to my alcoholic blathering...somewhat incoherently I suppose, but adequate enough in facts to bring Rodney up to date.

"Connie won't betray her mother and I can't betray Connie," I told Rodney, hoping for sympathy but expecting reproof. He put his hands in front of his face, the fingers touching, as if he were deep in thought. I was about to ring for a third drink when his face brightened and he said:

"You will hire a lawyer...the best that money can buy. The lawyer will launch an appeal based upon the fact that this Borman fellow was coerced into confessing. He will be released because everyone knows that the police are corrupt. No alternate version of the crime need be suggested. Hence, you ease your conscious and still protect the object of your affections."

"Brilliant! But who?"

"There is a lawyer in town named Clarence Darrow. He has been known to take on so-called lost causes. He defended Eugene Prendergast, the lunatic who murdered Mayor Carter Harrison and then walked into a police station and confessed."

"Prendergast was executed."

"But he is a champion of the poor, the weak, the weary. A friend of the working man. He defended Eugene V. Debs and members of the American Railway Union. You remember the strike of the clothing workers against Hart, Schafner and Marx? Darrow represented the workers in the agreement that finally was reached. Only last year he defended the MacNamara brothers out in Los Angeles who had set a bomb at the Los Angeles Times building because of the newspaper's anti-union stance."

"I read about that case," I said. "I also read that Darrow was indicted on two counts of jury bribery."

"He was acquitted. And so what? You admit that the police in this case have lied or at best withheld facts in order to save face. So what if one has to fight dishonesty with dishonesty?"

"I don't know, Rodney. A big union lawyer…is he going to take on our lost cause?"

"It can't hurt to ask. First though, you have to visit this Borman fellow. Get him to agree to the appeal."

"I will. I'll try to talk to him. You think they'll let me in to see him?"

"Why not? Just don't try to smuggle in a file in a cake or anything. By the way, any more ideas on the mystery of the locked room? Are you ready for me to reveal the solution?"

"Not now, Rodney. I've too much on my mind. I have to save an innocent man from the gallows and try to revive an unrequited love affair."

"Most probably the former will be easier than the latter."

The jail was two buildings, the old jail and the new, although the distinction was lost on me. It was just north of the Hubbard Street courthouse on West Illinois Street, between Clark and Dearborn. One commuted between the jail and the courthouse via an enclosed bridge suspended across the alleyway. There were departments, segregated of course, for men, women, and juveniles. There were one hundred and ten cells in four tiers in the men's area, with seven tiers in all. The tiers in the new jail were connected by another iron bridge to the old jail. The old jail was the where executions took place. If you had someone to open all the locked doors in route for you, you could easily move from the courtroom to the gallows—as I was afraid would happen to Slippery Willy.

I entered at the Dearborn Street entrance and went immediately to the Chief Jailer's office on the first floor. The Chief Jailer was a man named Oliver Whitman. I anticipated difficulty with my petition to speak to Willy Borman, but Chief Whitman was cordial and even offered to give me a brief tour of his jail. I didn't want to take the time to do this, but the man was obviously proud of his institution and probably also starved for the company of anyone not connected to the penal system.

It seemed unsanitary and overcrowded to me even though pundits raved about its modern facilities: the cells were fitted with wash basins and toilets and were well ventilated. Four of the cells, referred to by the guards as "dungeons," were used for unruly prisoners and were as dark as the Black Hole of Calcutta, that terrible place where Siraj ud-Daulah smothered British prisoners after the fall of Fort William.

There were two hospital wards, many shower rooms and some tubs, essential to preserving the health and cleanliness of the incarcerated population. But for the preservation of their mental health I saw only very short stretches of hallway on each tier which were called "bull-pens" in which, once released from their cells, they could recreate. The only exercise possible, however, was to form a line and circle around the corridor while avoiding collisions with the more stationary prisoners. Most leaned despondently against the walls as far from the open drain, which was used as a urinal, as possible. Chief Whitman led me back to the first floor to arrange for my visitation with Borman.

From a speaking tube in his office, Whitman summoned a guard and assigned the man to guide me to the fourth floor where the cells of the condemned were located. There were elevators leading up to the tiers. Here I got a closer look at the living conditions of the prisoners. The cells were built of steel with a barred grating at one end and a small, solid, sliding steel door at the other. A single light bulb was the only illumination. Beds were attached to the walls like bunks, and consisted of a straw-filled mattress and a thin blanket, sheet and pillow. There was a toilet and a wash basin. I saw filth, litter from uneaten food, and rats.

We reached Willy Borman's cell. The guard unlocked the door, ushered me in and slid the door shut with a loud metallic clanging sound which reminded me of the descent of the blade of a French guillotine. I introduced myself and said that I was a friend; Willy Borman simply stared into space in front of himself. Of course, why should he trust a stranger like me?

"I witnessed your trial and I was deeply affected by the unfair treatment you had at the hands of the prosecution and the judge. I believe you are innocent and I want to help you."

At this, Willy Borman stood up from the bunk where he sat and came closer to me. He spoke with a rough, gravely voice within inches of my ear: "Why you would help such as me?"

"You can call me a crusader if you like. An altruistic do-gooder. A bleeding-heart liberal (this was as far from the truth as could be, but I needed to gain Borman's confidence). They are going to hang you for a crime you didn't commit...isn't that reason enough?"

"I'm gonna swing all right. And soon! If you can do anything...it better be before Tuesday next, or you can bring flowers for my grave."

I placed a hand on the man's shoulder. "If you'll allow it, I will pay for a good lawyer and we will make an appeal. I think it can be shown that the police beat that confession out of you. The rest was circumstantial evidence or no evidence at all. We'll get to pick a jury of your peers...working men, not bored office men who would as soon spit on you as look at you. Let me help you."

Willy Borman sat slowly back on the bed, his hands cradling his face. There might have been tears forming in his eyes, but I couldn't see. I banged on the door for the guard. He took his time coming to let me out. Those moments were among the most frightening of my life. Locked in an iron box! Perhaps I *was* becoming a crusader.

8

The Appeal

The law offices of Clarence Darrow were in the Monadnock Building at 53 West Jackson Boulevard. It seemed appropriate for a dedicated man with few personal frills such as Darrow to be housed in an atypically unadorned structure like the Monadnock. Named for a mountain in New Hampshire, the Monadnock block consisted of two narrow "skyscrapers" of 16 and 17 stories which had been erected between 1889 and 1893. The north-most building was the last, highest all-masonry, load-bearing building built before restricting codes were enacted requiring steel framing; the ground floor walls were six feet thick and the foundation extended 11 feet beyond the building's footprint.

I walked through the district they called "Printing House Row," past other monuments to human ingenuity and commercial prowess. Past the Manhattan Building, the Old Colony Building, and the Fisher Building—the works of gifted and innovative architects. Unlike these worthy structures, the Monadnock was devoid of ornament, presenting a massive geometry of stone not unlike the pyramids of old Egypt in its severity and purity. The slightly inward tapering of the lower stories added to the effect. Yet in contrast to this simplicity, each floor ended in pairs of four-windowed bays which jutted from the blankness of the red granite and purplish-brown brick. These alternated with narrow slits of recessed windows giving a needed modularity to the building's surface.

I entered the lobby, walked past the marbled stairs with their lacey aluminum railings, the only nod to extravagance in this minimalistic environment, and waited at the bank of elevators. In moments I was rising rapidly toward the fourteenth floor. When I stepped out into the corridor I was pleasantly surprised at the amount of light streaming from the feather-chipped glass transoms of the offices on either side and the great bay windows at the hallway's end. There were no offices without outside windows and glassed transoms so if one expected the darkness of a tomb to reside at the interior of that massive sculptural edifice…well, one was surprised.

Clarence Seward Darrow sat behind his desk; he had not bothered to stand up when I entered the office and seemed engrossed in reading a thick law book that lay open before him. He wore no jacket, his shirt sleeves were rolled up (the shirt crumpled as if it had not been ironed), but his bowtie was expertly and neatly tied at his neck. The red suspenders and the wisp of hair falling across his forehead completed his semblance to a country bumpkin—but Darrow was no hick! It was true he had been born into a poor Ohio family and had been mostly self-educated. He was like a modern-day Abe Lincoln, but stout and hefty instead of skinny like a rail. And he was a brilliant trail lawyer.

I explained my purpose in seeking his assistance in the Dunning murder case. I told him as much of the truth as I dared, leaving out Connie's admission of her mother's guilt. I stressed the injustice of saddling the poor man with an incompetent attorney—this fact seemed to pique Darrow's interest. I pointed out the judge's refusal to allow testimony against the malfeasance of the police. I spoke of the details the police detective had omitted (the voices Irene Dunning had heard) and of the fabrications he had used to tie the crime to Slippery Willy (the "fleeing" assailant). I hoped I had painted a picture of a persecuted man who desperately needing salvation.

Darrow's eyebrows arched. "What I am wondering," he said, "is what you are not telling me. Why are you so interested in reversing this miscarriage of justice. Justice…hmmph. Justice is never found in courtrooms. Justice is what comes out of courtrooms.'

"I'm not sure I understand. Are you interested in the case at all?"

"Well, it doesn't sound very challenging. Any good lawyer…and I assume that doesn't include that public defender...should be able to mount an appeal that would expose the irregularities in the trial. What about proving the man's innocence, however?"

"Isn't he innocent until proven guilty?"

"He has been proven guilty. What we have to do now is unprove it. An alternate theory of the crime could produce reasonable doubt. The voices that were heard arguing, for instance. If we knew the identities of these..."

"I have no idea about that. I think it is a dead end. Can't we just overturn the verdict? Wouldn't that be enough to release the man?"

"No idea? That's a shame because it would certainly be a lynch pin...if you'll excuse the expression...toward winning our case."

"Then you'll defend him? I'll pay of course. And you won't need the alternate theory?"

"You're tying my hands. But yes, I'll take the case. By the way, is she pretty?"

It was a different courtroom; this one had a mural of the trading post operated by Chicago's first settler, a free-black from Haiti named Jean Baptiste DuSable. DuSable was shown in front of a modest cabin surrounded by Native Americans, French and British soldiers and buckskinned explorers, presumably his customers. There was also a different judge, a younger man without facial hair and what Shakespeare would have called a lean and hungry look. His name was Judge Norman P. Winthrop (the Honorable). One hoped the "P" stood for Peace.

The Assistant State's Attorney was a different person as well. Lloyd Waters, Darrow told me later, was high up the pecking order within the State's Attorney's office. He had been hand-picked for this retrial by his boss, Cook County State's Attorney, Maclay Hoyne. This was a good thing, Darrow said, because Hoyne had engaged in a personal and professional vendetta to rid Chicago of police corruption and political conspiracy. He had obtained convictions against, for instance, William Stine, head of police organization, who had embezzled a portion of a secret police slush fund, Edward Jones, an attorney who fixed witnesses, Seymour Simpson, a city official who shook down venders, and many police officers on the take.

When I commented that we were in luck having Hoyne's right-hand man as our opposition, Darrow shook his head and proceeded to list some of the notorious murder cases Hoyne had prosecuted and won: Paul Brencato who had severed the head of Joseph Minella, William Ellis who murdered his wife by cutting her throat, Ike Bond who had murdered Ida Leegson, the sculptress from the Art Institute, James Franche, AKA "Duffy the Goat," who was the Red Light District Killer, and the Conways, that circus clown and his wife who had been given so much attention in the newspapers for seducing and killing a young girl.

Rodney Morton and I sat in the first row of the spectator's section, immediately behind the long oak table where Clarence Darrow sat with his client, Willy Borman. I was astonished when Darrow turned and acknowledged Rodney; they knew each other! In what capacity, I wondered? Again I had to ponder Rodney's mysterious past, the past he never mentioned and wouldn't explain no matter how clever my probing. It became apparent later that Rodney was the reason Darrow had taken our case. A favor for an old friend.

Lloyd Waters, the prosecutor, outlined the circumstances of the murder and the capture of Slippery Willy during his opening statement. He would be presenting, he said, the signed confession as evidence of Willy's guilt. There was nothing surprising in this. Clarence Darrow seemed unconcerned; in fact, he made quite a show of clipping the end of a rather large cigar, rolling it between his fingers and lighting it—a bit of theatrics designed to distract the jury. It seemed that he had them well entertained. Darrow had expended substantial effort during jury selection to insure that we had 12 honest, working class men. Men who appreciated a good cigar.

I looked over my shoulder at the crowd in the spectator's section. I spotted Connie and her mother a few rows back. I didn't know if they had been called to testify for the prosecution as before or if they were here because, like me, they felt a deep sense of responsibility for the fate of a homeless man named Willy Borman. What that fate would be was going to play out in this courtroom in the next few hours. Now it was Darrow's turn to give an opening statement.

He rose slowly, placed his still smoldering cigar in an ash tray, removed his tweed sport coat and draped it ceremoniously over the back of his chair, unbuttoned his cuffs and pushed his shirt sleeves back, strolled across the courtroom like a farm boy on his way to school down a dirt road—I wouldn't have been surprised if he had kicked up dust as he went—and came to the jury box where he stood silently for a few moments, searching all the faces of the 12 men and true with an intense gaze, and then he began:

"Gentlemen of the jury, my name is Clarence Darrow. I am here to defend the poor soul you see seated there (he jestured toward Borman) and to help you make the only decision possible in this case…to dismiss it with prejudice! Prejudice toward an unfair system which allows the police and the courts to try and convict an *innocent man* with trumped up evidence!

"Look at this man closely. Do you not see the lines of worry on his face etched there from a life of poverty and despair…caused, I will tell you…caused by the loss of a job he held for many years, a job he lost when the bosses laid him and others like him off…fired and turned out into the cold, heartless world just to save a few dollars for the owners and the stock holders. Living from day to day, eating from garbage cans, sleeping in the cold until one day a brutal policeman, a cop on the beat, hauls him into the station house.

"He is kept in a small dark room with a singe light shining in his face. He is beaten with rubber hoses that leave no visible mark. He is threatened and humiliated and harassed until he affixes his signature on a document that is a lie from beginning to end. He signs to stop the beating, the yelling, the intimidation. He is taken to trial where the judge disallows testimony that would reveal his cruel treatment at the hands of the police. He is railroaded because this case…you see…this case is the case of the murder of a wealthy, powerful member of the elite…the movers and the shakers of industry…the very same types that closed down the factory where he had worked for a barely living wage. The police, who were too incompetent to actually solve a murder case, needed a pasty. William Borman, a common man who has fallen on hard times…this could happen to you or me…stands before you now asking for justice. Thank you for your attention and I know you will do the right thing."

The country boy act was a magnificent masquerade—this man was a giant intellect and a masterful manipulator. I was heartened by the performance Darrow had laid before the jury. Certainly Willy Borman would be breathing fresh air at the end of the trial! But that trial had to proceed through all its rituals, including the monotony of testimony, objections and sustainments, the gaveling when the spectators murmured too loudly—this occurred when Detective

Lieutenant Andrew Clancy insisted the questioning of Willy Borman had been aboveboard and respectful. On the heels of this minor courtroom commotion, Clarence Darrow rose to cross examine the good Lieutenant.

"Detective Clancy," Darrow began, "you deny that the suspect, William Borman, was in any way treated brutally in order to obtain a confession, is that correct?"

"Absolutely. We handled him with kid gloves."

"More like rubber gloves, I imagine. Can you enlighten us, Inspector, as to how it was that you selected my client, a poor indigent homeless man, as the object of your investigation? Was he acting suspiciously? Did he attempt to elude capture?"

"We were aware of Slippery Willy's criminal behavior in the past. He appeared to be a logical suspect."

"How many other logical suspects did the police arrest at that time?"

"Just Slippery Willy."

"I see. Now, Detective Clancy, when you arrived at the murder scene you met Mrs. Dunning. Did you question her about the incident?"

"She said she had discovered the body."

"Did she not say that she had heard the voices of two men arguing with her husband just before the murder took place?"

"I don't recall. I would have to check my notes."

"Do you have your notes with you? Very good. Would you please look through them now?"

Clancy pulled one of those cheap, imitation alligator notebooks from his inside jacket pocket and ruffed through it. "Nope. Nothing here about that."

"Detective, please be certain you answer this next question with absolute certainty of the facts: did not Mrs. Dunning say that no one had been in the room when she entered *immediately after hearing her husband fall to the floor*, and that she had seen no one leaving the house?"

Again Clancy consulted his notebook. Again he expressed ignorance of Irene Dunning's statement. Darrow turned toward the jury and shook his head as if to say, "What a liar!" I was fairly certain the jury took it all in.

After the prosecution rested, Darrow called his witnesses: Mrs.

Dunning and Connie. Both contradicted Lieutenant Clancy's statement. I was a bit nervous about his coming so close to the truth, that the murderer had to be a family member, but casting a reasonable doubt in the jurors' minds was a necessary tactic. Darrow was treading precariously along a path that could lead to disaster for Irene Dunning. However, his next witness focused on the gist of the defense—the malfeasance of the police.

"Call William Borman!"

Willy Borman took the stand. An accused man need not testify, of course, but Darrow had to establish that Willy's confession had been coerced. I watched the jurors' faces as Willy described his ordeal at he hands of the police interrogators. Not a few of the jury winced as if they were feeling those very blows Willy had endured. It would have been difficult not to experience empathy for Willy as he told of the blurred vision, the swinging ceiling lamp that felt like the burning of a thousand suns, the rush of urine at the final bludgeoning…the desperation that forced a false confession…

"I just wanted it to stop! I would have said anything!" Here Willy tried, but was unable to inhibit a series of pitiful sobs. The jury was moved. The whole courtroom was moved. What clinched it for us was Assistant District Attorney Lloyd Waters' cross examination which followed before Willy tears were even dry. Waters attempted to brow beat Borman into retracting his statement. The timbre of his raised voice seemed to echo the scene of the alleged intimidation of the prisoner and reinforced our defense better than any testimony ever could. I was certain we had won. The defense rested.

"Attorney Waters," said Judge Winthrop, "are you ready for your summation?"

"Your Honor," Waters replied, "if it may please the court, we have one more piece of evidence crucial to this case we would like to enter at this time."

Waters handed an envelope to the bailiff, who walked to the bench and handed it to the judge. Judge Winthrop opened the envelope and inspected its contents. He handed it back to the bailiff and said, "Very well, you may proceed."

"Your Honor," Darrow complained, "I object to the introduction of evidence not in the initial disclosure."

"This apparently has been some time in preparation. You may examine the evidence now. Bailiff, please give that envelope to Mr.

Darrow."

Rodney and I craned our necks to look over Darrow's shoulder as he opened the envelope. Inside were two sheets of paper upon which were black smudges. "Finger prints!" exclaimed Rodney.

"Your Honor, I wish to enter into evidence these two sheets of paper. The first is a set of finger prints taken from the scene of the murder. On the second are the prints taken from the defendant when he was arrested and booked. We have had an expert examine them and he will testify that they are identical. This places the defendant at the scene of the crime and substantiates his confession."

"Objection! Finger prints are at best the flimsiest form of evidence. There is no statute allowing such evidence. Why are these just now coming to light?" Darrow was fuming.

"Your honor, I call your attention to the State against Thomas Jennings in the murder of Clarence Hiller in this very city in 1910. Finger prints were used in the conviction which was subsequently upheld by the Supreme Court in the appeal." Waters was grinning broadly.

Things had taken a turn for the worse. Now, to my surprise, Darrow turned to Rodney and handed him the two finger print sheets. "What do you see?" he asked.

Rodney scrutinized the two sets of finger prints. "Why, they are identical," he said. "No wait…they *are* identical! This second sheet is a copy of the first. See, the exact smears of ink show on the thumb print. It's a trick!"

Before Darrow could bring this extraordinary sham to the attention of the judge, a new commotion was occurring in the back of the courtroom. Judge Winthrop's gavel was descending with loud cracks. An uproar had started as police scuffled with two men trying to work their way up to the bench. It was with great apprehension and alarm that I recognized Peter Dunning and Sammy Kaminsky! Sammy broke free and rushed up to the judge. "It was me!" he cried. "I did it!"

"Order! Order in the court!" shouted the judge. "You did what, young man?"

"I killed Willard Dunning. This man had nothing to do with it. It was me."

Then Peter Dunning, panting, approached. "No, judge. *I* did it," he said. "I killed my father. I hit him with a statue. I didn't mean it…I lost my temper."

"Hold on, everyone. Am I to believe we now have *three* confessions to this heinous crime?"

Suddenly, the one thing that could have made things worse happened. After all the effort to avoid implicating her, Irene Dunning rose from her seat and declared, "I did it. I killed my husband!"

Judge Norman P. Winthrop threw up his hands in desperation. "I hereby declare this to be a mistrial. The police are ordered to take all *four* of these so-called confessed murderers into custody and to get to the bottom of this once and for all. And Detective Clancy, you are admonished to conduct this new investigation with all prudence and care and to document all interviews…which will be done under the supervision of counsel. Court dismissed!"

9

The Fifth Suspect

Judge Winthrop had issued a decision vacating the conviction in the first trial of Willy Borman. Willy was still being held as a suspect but at least he had gotten off Murderers' Row. Sammy and Peter were in the general lockup at the County Jail but in deference to her womanhood, Irene Dunning was released on her own cognizance. Detective Lieutenant Andrew Clancy had been replaced as chief investigator in the matter of the murder of Willard Dunning. The case had been taken over by Captain Mathew Powers.

Powers was by all counts a gifted administrator. He had come up through the ranks from beat officer to detective and ultimately settled into the comfortable desk job of overseeing the daily operation of the North Side District of Chicago. That he was qualified to lead the investigation was not in doubt, nor was his reputation for honesty and integrity. He had reviewed Clancy's sparse notes and the transcripts from both trials. He had conducted initial interviews with the four suspects. And he had given the matter his utmost attention and deepest reasoning.

Captain Powers reasoned that Willy Borman was undoubtedly a patsy and that his confession had been obtained via the usual underhanded police methods. Scratch Willy Borman. Powers also reasoned that Sammy Kaminsky had confessed in order to save Willy

Borman and that Peter Dunning had confessed to save his friend, Sammy Kaminsky. It followed, therefore, that Irene Dunning had confessed in order to save her son, Peter. The only person with likely knowledge of the crime but who had not confessed was Constance Dunning.

Connie became the fifth, and to Captain Powers' way of thinking, the most likely suspect.

It was unseasonably warm for November. On Election Day, the thermometer hit 57 degrees. President Taft had not been supported at the polls as he had expected—Teddy Roosevelt's Bull Moose Progressive Party had pulled away many Republican voters, enough to put him in second place behind Democrat Woodrow Wilson. Wilson won the election by a landslide. Vice President James Sherman had died only a few days before the election which also hadn't helped matters for Taft. Now there was going to be a new president and, it was being reported, a Federal Income Tax! What other monumental changes were in store for us, I wondered?

Clarence Darrow declined representing any of the five suspects. He had been called away to defend striking coal miners in the east. He was still recoiling from his ordeal in California where he had been indicted for bribing jury members. This might be the last labor-related campaign he would be asked to pursue as the union bosses were becoming distrustful of him. "No other offense has ever been visited with such severe penalties," Darrow said, "as seeking to help the oppressed."

I conferred with Rodney as was my custom. "This is no longer your responsibility," he pointed out. "The Dunnings certainly can afford legal counsel of high merit…and most probably high expense."

"But your expertise in legal matters, which I might add, is just coming to light for me, could help steer them in the right direction. It is pretty obvious that either Connie or her mother will be charged, although for the life of me I can't see where they will get any evidence unless they manufacture it again."

"Or if Connie either confesses or testifies against her mother."

"And we can't get Darrow. Isn't there anyone you can suggest that is at least a fraction as brilliant as he?"

"Darrow had a law partner until a few years ago named Edgar Lee Masters. He opened his own law firm after breaking with

Darrow...some kind of personality conflict I think. But I don't know if he is still practicing. They say he is pursuing a literary career...poetry of all things."

"And you know him...from the old days?" I was probing again, hoping the Rodney would reveal something about his past, but he changed the subject.

"You need to let this go. At least until the police either release everyone or charge them. How about one of my made-up mysteries. I have one where there are these ten people on an island..."

"Rodney," I said, becoming annoyed with the man who had entertained me with his puzzles in the past but now wished to perplex me with insoluble riddles—and just at a time when real life had thrown at me a dilemma of such magnitude that my head ached just to think about it. "Rodney, you've never told me the solution to the locked room. Impossible murders are not just very popular with me right now."

"See here old fellow, you never asked the right questions about that one. Exercise that gray matter between your ears for a bit. It will take your mind off of your troubles."

I stretched out, my feet on the ottoman. It was inevitable. The game was to be afoot.

"Okay. Let's see if I remember correctly. The murder victim was slumped over his desk, a bullet hole in his forehead, a pool of blood spreading slowly on the green felt blotter. The only door to the room was bolted from the inside. The maid had seen the man enter his study and close and lock the door. When the man didn't respond to her knocking she summoned the son who broke down the door. He sent the maid for the police. There was no murder weapon found in the room and the only window was also bolted from the inside."

"That sums it up nicely."

"I still think it was a suicide and the son removed the gun after the maid left but before the police arrived. He stood to inherit the proceeds of a large insurance policy, but the company wouldn't pay if the man had taken his own life."

"That's a good guess, but it isn't the solution."

"It wasn't a suicide?"

"It wasn't a suicide. It was definitely a murder. Who did it and how did they do it?"

"And why was it rigged up to look like an impossible murder in a locked room?"

Precisely. Who stood to gain?"

"Well, obviously not the maid...unless...was she the man's mistress who was the actual beneficiary of the insurance policy?"

"Why do you think there was an insurance policy? Does the motive for murder always need be monetary?"

"No, just like our own murder...the Dunning murder. A crime of passion, so to speak." As I said this I could see that Rodney was displeased that his attempt to distract me from my obsession with the Dunning murder had gone awry.

"There is no point in supplying you with the answer at this juncture," Rodney said, nearly growling at me. "Murder may be committed as a passionate response to some overwhelming situation, but there must also be a predestined motivation, a propensity toward virulence. Fear, hatred, jealousy, ambition...how ever many deadly sins you wish to recount can predispose the actor to his or her action."

"That is an amazingly dismal outlook, if you don't mind me saying so. What about the desire to protect, to prevent harm to another? A defensive burst of strength to ward off an impending threat of violence or coercion? An accident of force in reaction to..."

"A catharsis? The deeply seated but repressed emotion of *fear, hatred, jealousy or ambition!*"

When I left the Jefferson League Club that day with Rodney's words still fresh in my mind, I wondered exactly to which murder they applied—the fictional locked room mystery or the much too real Dunning murder case? I arrived home, kicked off my shoes and immediately settled into my chair in the second floor turret room. The trees outside my window were buffeted by the strong wind off Lake Michigan. There was a squirrel nest high up in one of the elms that swung and bobbed—impossibly stuck onto the end of a long, leafless branch. I feared for the squirrel. I feared for my friends, in peril under an inquisition by the police.

George Mandel, my butler, entered my sanctum sanctorum. His age caused him to walk with intermittent pauses, like the squirrel that lived in my tree hoping across a lawn after a nut. I barely noticed him. He cleared his throat and said, "Sir, there is a young lady downstairs wishing to see you."

Connie! My malaise turned to jubilation. I slid my feet into a pair of leather slippers and practically bounded down the stairs. But when I reached the foyer it was not Connie who was waiting for me; Alicia Kaminsky stood twisting her bonnet in clenched hands, inquietude and unease spoiling her otherwise pretty face.

"It's Sammy," she blurted. "He's still in the jail house. Peter had a lawyer come and bail him out, but Sammy has no money for lawyers. And that woman…I think she is going testify against him!"

"You mean Irene Dunning? She's going to say Sammy killed her husband?"

"No…the other woman. The daughter."

Why would Connie claim Sammy was the murderer? Of course…to protect her brother and her mother. She wouldn't care what happened to Sammy! The police must be closing in on the truth. I had to help.

"We'll go right now and bail him out. I know of a lawyer that I think will help us. Wait while I get my shoes."

I had hoped never again to have to visit that dreadful jail. We waited in Oliver Whitman's office on the first floor. The Chief Jailer had a collection of death masks of criminals who had been executed at the Chicago jail which he displayed on a high shelf above his desk. I hadn't noticed these on my first visit and wished I hadn't noticed them this time either. Alicia was particularly disturbed by the array of grimacing faces with their unnaturally closed eyes. I turned her away from the sight while we awaited the release of her brother.

I had paid for Sammy Kaminsky's bail and I would be paying this new attorney's fees should his help be needed, although I hadn't contacted anyone as yet. Alicia had been reluctant to accept my financial assistance at first, but I was able to convince her that the seriousness of Sammy's situation overruled any shame she might feel about receiving what was essentially charity. This charity, as I was reluctant to characterize it, was merely an act of good will on my part. The truth was I still had enormous feelings of guilt knowing I was motivated primarily to protect Connie and possibly, her mother.

Chief Jailer Whitman returned with Sammy in shackles. He retrieved a set of keys from his desk drawer, found the correct key and released Sammy. "Here, you must sign this receipt," Whitman told me. "Remember, you lose your bail money if the suspect skips town."

"That won't happen. And I'll point out that he hasn't been charged with anything formally. You really can't hold him more than 48 hours without charging him with a crime."

"Fleeing the scene of a murder is what I hear tell is the charge."

I knew it was useless to fight City Hall, as the expression goes, so I signed the document and we hurried away from that glorified dungeon as fast as our legs could carry us. No one said anything as I drove to Mount Pleasant. At the house, Alicia asked me to come inside. I was glad for this for several reasons, not the least of which was a desire to spend some time with the girl. Also I was eager for an opportunity to ask some pointed questions of young Master Kaminsky.

This was the first time I had seen Sammy Kaminsky up close. He was slight of build, so slight that I doubted he would have had the strength to knock Willard Dunning's brains out, no matter what the weapon. I had to know, however, what his version of the crime was. I had to convince him it was too late to protect anyone...the truth was the only logical course of action. I started with an obvious inquiry, one that would give the impression I supported him:

"Why do you think Constance Dunning would be accusing you of the murder? What could she possibly say without lying?"

"She wants to put the blame on someone else. Someone not in the family."

"Yes, I see that. But what could she say? She told the police she saw no one. And if suspicion is cast upon you, won't it also fall on Peter?"

"Peter and I had a horrible argument with his father in the living room. Mr. Dunning stormed upstairs and shut himself in his study. Connie went up to try to reason with him. We didn't think it was a good idea and we tried to keep her from making things worse, but she went to him anyway. We could hear her and her father yelling at each other all the way downstairs."

"Wait a minute, you weren't in the study with Mr. Dunning before he was killed?"

"Not at all. Then Mrs. Dunning went upstairs as well. Peter followed her up but came back down a few minutes later white as a sheet. 'We've got to go. Now!' he told me. We ran down the street and caught a bus. We sat way in the back, away from the other riders and that's when he told me."

"His father had been murdered. And you think either Connie or her mother…"

"When we heard that a man had been arrested and put on trial for the murder…well, we knew he couldn't have done it. We hurried back to Chicago and when we got to the courtroom, I just panicked. I didn't think. I yelled out that I had done it."

"Then Peter. Then his mother. One more question…how did you learn that Connie might testify against you?"

"The police told me. Peter and I both retracted our confessions once we were taken to the jail. They questioned us relentlessly."

"And without counsel present as usual. Don't you think maybe it was a tactic to get you to confess again? Or to get you to put the blame on someone else?"

"I wouldn't admit anything. I told them I saw nothing…which was true. Peter didn't tell anything either. The problem is that Mrs. Dunning told the police she had heard voices arguing. Logically it was Peter and I arguing with Mr. Dunning."

"And everyone is telling a different story. By the way, is there really a secret panel in that study?"

"A what? No…I don't…I haven't the faintest idea."

December was almost as mild as November had been. There were one or two cold snaps but weather in the 40s and 50s suggested there would not be a white Christmas this year. Just as well. I was comfortable watching the squirrel nest swinging in the wind from my vantage point in the turret room. But I was getting stir-crazy. A drive in the country would raise my spirits…or so I thought.

The Overland was garaged at the end of the block in an old horse barn that I had been able to rent for the purpose. There was a canvas top for the roadster which afforded some small protection from rain but was open on the sides. It would serve to block most of the wind, particularly if I unfolded the windscreen so that it reached up to the front of the canvas top. Someday, I thought, automobiles would come equipped with kerosene heaters for these blustery days.

There was still one additional element necessary to secure the perfection of my desired recreational excursion: companionship. What was the use of rolling meadows and gentle hillocks when a person was the singular observer of such tranquility? I considered asking Alicia Kaminsky to join me in my jaunt through the countryside. Blond hair and blue eyes would complete the enchantment I sought. But then something devious in the unsettled marrow of my being evoked that other anima, that femme fatale who occupied my most worrisome thoughts: Constance Dunning.

"You've been avoiding me," she said as I helped her up into the Overland. She had wrapped her body in a warm cloak and wound a long knitted scarf around her neck which dragged on the ground. This made me think of Isadora Duncan who always wore long flowing scarves. I insisted that Connie gather the loose end of the scarf up and hold it on her lap. I didn't wish it to be caught in the wheels of the automobile!

"I haven't been avoiding you," I replied. "I was just giving you some space, so to speak. I am at your service whenever you may have need of me, you know that."

We headed out Ogden Avenue to reach the limits of the city as swiftly as possible. Cities maintained their own roadways, of course, but the country roads were engineered and developed under the auspices of the counties and varied from rutted dirt to crushed stone to macadam—although the latter was in short supply. There were still some of the old plank roads in existence, but these had fallen into disrepair and their splinters could shred rubber tires in an instant. As more and more people now owned motor vehicles, the interest in good roads was mounting and state and county governments were apt to create legislation for the general improvement of the byways very soon. I'd even read of a plan to designate a so-called transcontinental highway stretching from Times Square in New York City all the way to Lincoln Park in San Francisco!

My intended route would take us on fair roads west to the city of Aurora, then north along the Fox River to Geneva, Illinois, a distance of over 40 miles. There we could have a late lunch before motoring back. The scenery would be inspiring, even in early winter. The farmland was flat but broken by wooded areas, rivers and the occasional small town. There had been a plank road along this route, but it was long gone, the wood scavenged for out-buildings and fences.

"I have to ask you, Connie," I said, once we were past the traffic of the city (most of which consisted of horse-drawn wagons loaded with everything from lumber to cabbages), "has anyone been charged yet?"

"That poor man they arrested at first has been released. No one is being held, but the questioning is becoming more and more pointed."

"How do you mean?"

"They ask me to go over it again and again until...I can't remember what I've said and haven't said."

"What have you said?" I needed to know if indeed she had implicated Sammy Kaminsky. There were too many versions of the story now, and I wondered which one, if any, the police were considering.

"I don't know...but...I think they suspect my mother! I told you she had done it, but I never even hinted to the police..."

"But certainly there isn't any proof one way or another. Without an actual eye witness. And you didn't see the act. If the boys were in the room..."

"No, they weren't. They stayed downstairs and mother went up."

According to Sammy Kaminsky, it was Connie who had climbed the stairs to her father's study. I didn't understand why she was still lying to me. I decided, then and there, to seek out the lawyer Rodney had told me about. I had a feeling Irene Dunning would be needing one. And soon.

10

The Poet Lawyer

I had sought an interview with the lawyer, Edgar Lee Masters, on the advice of my friend Rodney Morton. Masters had an office in the Marquette Building on South Dearborn Street. I spent a little time admiring the bas reliefs at the entry depicting Father Jacques Marquette's exploration of the Great Lakes—Chicagoans are forever immortalizing their historical forbearers in marble and bronze and with mosaics of sparkling glass. In the lobby were more murals of Marquette's life and legend; these by Louis Comfort Tiffany in favrile glass, abalone mother-of-pearl and what looked like lapis lazuli, sun stone and serpentine.

Rodney had told me much about Masters. He had made his acquaintance years ago at the Everleigh Club (where many business meetings were combined with pleasure). Apparently Masters was a womanizer. The knowledge that the attorney was a devotee of all things erotic didn't surprise me, nor did it discourage me. It made him out to be human and a realist, two attributes I felt would aid our cause. Upon presenting myself at the law office, however, I was told that Masters had taken the day to work at home.

I knew from Rodney's recital of Master's recent history that he had been besotted with a woman who was not his wife. He had, from feelings of guilt, and no doubt a keen sense of political acumen where wife-placating was concerned, bought an expensive, three-story Georgian mansion that his spouse had insisted she could not live without (his wife's name was Helen) on Kenwood Avenue in the stylish Hyde Park area of Chicago's South Side. It was there I would meet the reluctant lawyer and would-be poet, Edgar Lee Masters.

Helen Masters ushered me into the parlor where an over-stuffed chair accommodated my travel-weary body; I had taken buses and trolleys instead of hiring a cab; sitting on those rigid seats had taken its toll. While the woman went to summon his nibs I perused a volume of verse that sat on an occasional table near my chair. It was entitled "Songs and Sonnets by Webster Ford." I knew that Webster Ford was a pseudonym that Masters had used. Being a poet was bad for business in the practice of law, he would later tell me. My eye fell on the last verse of a poem called "Eternal Woman." It seemed somehow apropos.

> *She is the mystery of the world*
> *Strayed out from heaven above.*
> *The light that lures beyond the sky*
> *The souls foredoomed to rove.*
> *And if she slay us it is well,*
> *For she is Life and Love.*

And another from a poem with the ominous title of "Love is a Madness":

> *LOVE is a madness, love is a fevered dream,*
> *A white soul lost in a field of scarlet flowers—*
> *Love is a search for the lost, the ever vanishing gleam*
> *Of wings, desires and sorrows and haunted hours.*

Did it cause me to reflect upon my own obsession with the fate of my "eternal woman," Connie Dunning? It should have, but it did not. I thought the poetry was a trifle démodé...moldy even. I preferred the more modern, imagist verses of Erza Pound or that new fellow who had a poem in Poetry Magazine, Carl Sandburg. I thought it advisable that Masters not quit his day job. In fact, I was beginning to wonder if I was making a mistake in soliciting the legal expertise of a man with a secret leaning toward the antithesis of logic and fact: his kind of anachronistic romanticism.

It was a comfortable room, but not without a certain stylistic conflict of appointments. Heavy drapes, a spindly old gas chandelier recently converted to electricity, a well worn oriental rug and a potted fern that spoke of the late Victorian; but a plain white oak writing desk with straight, squared legs, prominent iron hinges and drawer pulls upon which sat a pair of copper lamps with triangular glass shades suggested the modern movement called the Mission Style. It was a room in transition: reluctant to relinquish its roots but bravely entering the future, albeit in baby steps with a simple wooden bookshelf here, a straight-backed hand-crafted chair there.

Edgar Lee Masters entered the parlor; I stood up to shake his hand. I knew that he and Clarence Darrow had been partners not so long ago but that was difficult to visualize. Where Darrow hid sophistication and eloquence beneath a farm boy façade, Masters disguised his tortured poet's soul with an exterior of business-like formality that imbued seriousness; he was all pomp and circumspection and gave no clue as to his camouflaged secret persona.

"I have been limiting my legal activity of late," he told me, "but Rodney Morton spoke highly of you and told me of your dilemma. I must say, however, with the accused not yet identified, it does complicate matters."

"You know Rodney from…the old days?" I could not pass up an opportunity to discover something…anything…about my mysterious friend. Masters of course changed the subject:

"I haven't much experience defending clients accused of murder. I'm more used to litigation of a commercial nature. But I will take your case, when and if one or more of your friends is indicted. As a favor to Rodney. But be aware of the fact that it is a *society* murder. There will be a clamor for justice and a great interest in the case by the public. The unwritten law may not help us."

"The unwritten law? What is that?"

"Because women don't yet have the vote, they are not allowed to serve on juries, as you know. An all male jury is incapable of keeping sentiment for the opposite sex out of their deliberation. They almost never convict a woman who has killed a man, no matter how gruesome the act. It is a sort of chivalry, born in the Deep South which has migrated to the North in recent years.

"Take the recent case of the Bernstein murder. Mrs. Bernstein shot and killed her husband while he was sleeping. They had been separated and there was evidence to the fact that she had been planning the murder for several days. Yet the defense argued extenuating circumstances…furore transitoria, or temporary insanity in layman's terms. Mr. Bernstein had treated his wife cruelly as if she were a white slave, it was argued. Although murdering a defenseless man in his sleep might seem a cowardly act, the jury believed she was insane at the time and further more that she had a justifiable right to kill her husband. They acquitted her."

I said that this seemed to be good news, as a case for temporary insanity could surely be made for Connie or her mother. Then I made the mistake of mentioning Clarence Darrow.

"That son of a bitch is the most detestable person in American history," Master roared. "He is a gray-eyed infidel! You know I turned him down the first time he offered me a partnership. He was not in good odor in Chicago. But, ah well…one needs the money."

"I'm sorry," I replied, "I wouldn't have mentioned him except for the fact that he did right by the poor vagrant that the police arrested at first."

"Oh, he's at his best when there are tears to be shed for human suffering. He poses as an altruist and as a friend of the oppressed, but I doubt he is either. He suffuses pathos and has just the right kind of a face for it…an old face. He was old when he was born!"

"But do you think," (now I tried to change the subject) "that this unwritten law might be brought into play, even though the case has a high profile?"

"At this very moment there are seven women in Chicago jails accused of murder. Two of them, I would characterize as serial killers. These include Mrs. Louise Vermilya, who poisoned at least nine persons, and Mrs. Louise Lindloff, who poisoned at least seven. This does not bode well for our own women."

"But surely…"

"The fact that an argument was heard is a point in our favor. It suggests a crime that was not premeditated and in fact might be an act of protection by the accused…even an accident. We will just have to wait and see what the State puts forth."

We wouldn't have long to wait, but we didn't know that quite yet. I proceeded to give a detailed account of the differing stories told me by the principals. I felt Masters could form his own opinion as to the guilt or innocence of each. I didn't believe that whatever his opinion, it would interfere with his defense of his client. His natural cynicism for the law—justice and law, he would tell me, are just fancy terms for the private ends and means—that cynical insight he had would shield him both from sentiment and from ethos. Guilty or not, his client would have a champion of the first order. And so to the four stories:

One: Mrs. Irene Dunning told that she heard what appeared to be two men in an argument with her husband who was upstairs in his study. She went to the kitchen to talk to the cook, then climbed the stairs to relate the dinner plans to her husband. She heard a thud, as if a body had fallen to the floor, entered the room and saw her husband lying in a pool of blood. There was no one else in the room. She called to her daughter who summoned the police almost immediately.

Two: Constance Dunning first claimed that her brother, Peter, and his friend, Sammy Kaminsky, had been arguing with her father who would not accept their somewhat unusual relationship (we need not enlighten the jury about this particular relationship, said Masters). Mr. Dunning stormed upstairs and shut himself in his study. The two boys followed the man upstairs and the three continued to argue. Connie went to the kitchen to get a glass of water for her mother who was also a witness to the preliminary argument. When she returned, her mother, distraught over the conflict, also went upstairs. Connie then heard a scream. She went to the study and upon entering saw her mother standing over Willard Dunning's body, a small statue in her hand. She helped Peter and Sammy leave through a secret door hidden by a bookshelf so that they would not be seen. She and her mother cleaned up and changed clothes and then called the police.

Three: Sammy Kaminsky told a very different story. He and Peter did have an argument with Willard Dunning in the living room. Mr. Dunning did storm upstairs and shut himself in his study. But, Sammy said, it was Connie who went upstairs to try to reason with her father. Sammy and Peter remained in the living room. They could hear her arguing with her father. Shortly thereafter, Mrs. Dunning also went upstairs. Peter then followed but returned minutes later and told Sammy to follow him as they fled from the house. Sammy didn't provide a theory as to which of the Dunnings might have done the deed.

Four: Connie Dunning changed her story to say that neither Peter nor Sammy had left the living room to follow Mr. Dunning to his study. Her mother, she said, did go upstairs and Connie later found her standing over the body as she had previously related.

I also told Masters of Rodney's observation of the bloody footprints leading from the desk toward the back of the room and then stopping. Rodney had theorized that there was a secret door by which the murderer or murderers had either entered or exited, or both. I made some remark about Rodney's keen ability to distill insights from sparse clues, hoping to steer the conversation in a direction whereby I might gain some insight into the nature of Rodney's past but, it seemed, I was doomed to perpetual ignorance on that account.

"Who do you suspect?" Masters asked of me.

"I'm of the opinion…not a strong one, mind you…that the son, Peter is the culprit," I replied. "He is the only one who has not given a version of the story. Each of the other players in this tragic drama would have a motive for protecting him. What do you think?"

"I think…that the police will arrest the mother. Hers is the only story that doesn't hold water. She enters the room and it is empty except for the corpse. They will think she is either lying or crazy."

"What about the secret panel?"

"Do the police know about that? I think not. But let us hope that she is charged."

'What? Why?"

"The unwritten law. She has a good chance of being acquitted. A temporarily insane woman—and we will show how she has been mistreated over the years—in a fit of uncontrollable passion, defends herself and tragically ends the life of her spouse. At least she didn't poison him!"

I stopped at the Jefferson League Club on the way home. I needed a drink. I slumped down in my usual chair after giving Rodney a nod. He would begin to quiz me about my meeting with Edgar Lee Masters in a moment, but not until after I was settled in with a Scotch and a cigar. Bruce arrived to take our orders.

"I going to try a brandy old-fashioned, Bruce," Rodney told him.

"That new member just down from Madison has interested me in the drink."

"*Brandy* old-fashioned? Sir, isn't an old fashioned made with bourbon whiskey? You know, a lump of sugar, Angostura bitters, lemon peel and a jigger of whiskey?"

"Usually. But in Wisconsin they use *Wisconsin brandy*. You know I hate that Kentucky bourbon. And throw in a cherry."

"I'll see what I can dig up. And you, Sir?" asked Bruce, turning to me with a look of consternation on his face. Was I going to order a Lime Ricky or a Horse's Neck or some other sugary libation he would be embarrassed to carry through the common room? I answered:

"Just my usual Scotch, thank you, Bruce. Rocks. Oh, and better add a twist of orange peel to that," I added to taunt the poor old fellow.

I brought Rodney up to date about my meeting with Edgar Lee Masters although somehow I suspected my narration was superfluous. Rodney seemed to see all, know all and, if not to speak all, at least to give the impression he was holding back some vital piece of information…saving it for a special moment when he would spring some brilliant leap of logic on me just to hear me say, "Ah hah!"

"What do you think of Masters' opinion that Mrs. Dunning will be arrested?" I asked.

"I think he has reasoned well. We can only hope the police see it that way. If Irene Dunning is willing to take the fall for her family, she has a better than 80 percent chance of beating the rap."

"You think so? Isn't it presumptuous to assume that juries are not so fickle that you can predict such an outcome?"

"I can give you some examples. I was just reading an article in the Times complaining about the inability of Chicago juries to convict women who have murdered men." He retrieved a folded newspaper from the table next to his chair and ruffled through it to find the right page.

"Mrs. Rena Morrow of Hyde Park, who is a poetess," he read, "was recently acquitted of her husband's murder. Her husband, who was an inventor, was felled by two bullets on his back porch…two, mind you, ruling out suicide. The couple had quarreled, which was common knowledge. The defense argued that Morrow had killed himself or had been killed by burglars. Mrs. Morrow was apparently too pretty to be sent to the gallows.

"A man named Webster Guerin was killed by Mrs. Dora McDonald, the wife of Michael McDonald who, you might know, was a very successful gambler about town for many years. Mrs. McDonald was having an affair with Guerin. He was about to break this off. Dora McDonald entered his office and shot him. The defense argued that he had shot himself during a scuffle in which he attempted to pistol-whip the woman. She was acquitted, of course.

"Then there was Lucille McLeod who killed William Nieman in a hotel downtown where the two where having an illicit liaison…she was, by the way, teen-aged. It was the usual story…the man was going to leave her for another woman. This, I should mention, was a sort of 'locked room mystery' as the hotel room door had to be broken down. Inside the girl lay seriously wounded while the man was found dead. She told the jury that Nieman had shot her and then shot himself. The jury believed her.

"And others. Mrs. Minnie Williams gassed her husband…she was acquitted. Mrs. Jane Quinn killed her third husband…and the first two had died under mysterious circumstances as well. She claimed the murder was done by a burglar. She was released. Estelle Stout, another teen-aged young woman, shot a man who was delivering a picture frame. They had argued over the price. And the jury…"

"Acquitted her. I get it, Rodney. Chicago juries don't like to convict women. It's the unwritten law." We sat silently for some moments, then I had to ask: "Who do *you* think killed Willard Dunning?"

"The only person not complicit in the murder was Irene Dunning. The others acted in concert. Remember the three sets of footprints? They converged upon the man in his study…I can't say which of them hefted the statue that struck the blow…maybe it was like slaying Caesar on the steps of the senate and they all took a turn at him. It doesn't matter. They slipped out through the secret door just as Mrs. Dunning came to investigate. The boys left the city and Connie remained in the house. The rest you know."

I was horrified at this assertion, but I saw that it was the most logical conclusion, given the slim, but irrefutable evidence of the footprints. The law of parsimony, the one that people called Occam's razor, said that given a large number of complex explanations, the simplest was the most preferable. And of course there was that famous statement by the master detective, Sherlock Holmes: "When you have eliminated the impossible, whatever remains, *however improbable*, must be the truth." But what was impossible here? That one person had made three sets of footprints which ended at a wall? Or that a kind and frail lady had bashed her husband's brains out with a statue of The Thinker? Or that three people could conspire to murder a dictatorial father in the name of true love?

As we sat contemplating the bits of fruit floating in our drinks, Bruce appeared, suddenly, as if he had been materialized by some prestidigitator's slight of hand. He handed Rodney a note. I watched as Rodney's previously dreamy gaze dissolved into a deep perplexity. He handed me the note. I read:

Samuel Kamnisky has just been arrested for the murder of Willard Dunning. Suggest we confer. —ELM

11

Back to Ducktown

Winter came on like a violent sneeze that had been suppressed too long; the town had held its finger under its nose during November and December, but now that January had arrived there was a triumphant blast of wind and snow that flew horizontally through the Loop, coating everything in crystal whiteness. The lake glazed over with a crust of silver that glistened in the winter sun.

I dearly wished to visit the Kaminsky household before the trial. My roadster would be useless until the city's snow removal teams hitched up their plows to their sturdy drays. However, where there is a will, as it is said, there is a way—I rented a horse and sled complete with driver and set off to Ducktown.

Mrs. Kaminsky greeted me at the door. "Alicia at work now," she told me. I told her it was she I had come to visit. I wanted to reassure her that her son would have the best defense money could buy—and I was paying for it so I was in a position to know. She echoed what Alicia had said to me, that they didn't want to take charity. I understood this, but I also understood that Sammy didn't stand a chance with a public defender. I tried to explain this to the woman but she just shook her head and mumbled something in Polish which I couldn't understand.

"He a good boy. They will see that he can not be murderer," she told me. I wasn't so sure.

Masters' and Rodney's theory that Mrs. Dunning would be

charged had proven wrong. I believed the police knew, that because of the unwritten law, the wife would never be convicted. Nor would the daughter. That left two suspects, the son and his underprivileged friend, Sammy Kaminsky. Who better to send to the gallows! Sammy needed all the help he could get. Charity? I had begun to realize that my feelings for Alicia went beyond sympathy. If I had been captivated by Connie Dunning, that obsession turned sour the more I learned about her…and her possible role in the murder of her father. Was I transferring my need for an object of affection from Connie to Alicia? Or had the barely acknowledged spark of romance I had I felt for Alicia finally burst into a bona fide flame?

"Will you please to stay for dinner? You can see Alicia when she come home from work."

"I'd be honored, Mrs. Kaminsky. Let me ask…how will Alicia get home in all this snow?"

"If buses not run then she walk." Mrs. Kaminsky had obviously not been outside today!

"I have a sled and driver waiting outside. I'll send him down to Field's to collect her," I offered.

I gave the driver an extra sawbuck and instructed him to be at the shipping and receiving department of Marshall Field promptly at 5:45 PM and to ask for Alicia Kaminsky. After bringing her to the house he could return to his place of business, then come back to Ducktown around 9:00 PM to take me home. He was delighted to have the business, and the extra tips.

"And Mr. Kaminsky?" I enquired.

"He stop at Bennie's for a drink most nights. We wait supper for him, unless he have many more…then we eat without him."

I hadn't yet had the pleasure of meeting Klaudiusz Kaminsky (his friends called him Claude). I would still have to wait to make his acquaintance. This would be one of those nights when the piercing cold and the whip-like wind and the waist-deep drifts of winter's worst snowfall of the year would necessitate just one more draft (and another, and another) at Bennie's.

Baby Bernice was fussing so Mrs. Kaminsky attended to her while I stayed in the parlor, once again glancing at framed photographs and knick-knacks. The boy, Stephen thundered down the stairs, stopping short of a tumble when he saw me.

"Hello, Mister," he said. "Did you bring your auto?"

"No, Stephen, the snow is too deep. Did you go to school today?"

"No school. Snow is too deep," he replied with a chuckle.

Stephen and I chatted about school, baseball, the snow storm and my Willy's Overland Roadster, passing the time most admirably for two such differently aged beings. I liked the lad; I might like becoming his uncle someday—and this frightening thought was strangely less problematic than I should have assumed it would be.

Alicia arrived about 6:30 and brought the sled driver into the house with her. She had offered him a cup of hot chocolate. She led him into the kitchen, plopped him down on a chair while she heated up some milk in a pan on the stove. I followed them into the kitchen; it was warm and inviting and Alicia's friendly presence made it nearly perfect. We had a lot to talk about, but I hesitated to discuss her brother's situation while the sled driver could hear us.

Mrs. Kaminsky entered to put the finishing touches on the dinner she had prepared for us: a red beetroot soup with potatoes, a kind of stew with kielbasa and sauerkraut, pickled cucumbers and strips of red peppers, and a carrot salad with granny smith apple slices. Seeing the sled driver, she immediately asked him to stay for the meal. The man, even as he sipped his hot chocolate, seemed embarrassed to have intruded into this domestic scene. He politely declined her offer, apologizing for tracking snow into her clean kitchen. The stark contrast between this mutual cordiality and the kind of reception the same man might have gotten at a place like the Dunning household was provocative—the image of this amiable gathering in the tiny kitchen would remain with me for a long time.

The meal underway, sans Mr. Kaminsky, I enumerated the positive qualities of attorney Edgar Lee Masters, trying to portray a rosy picture of the outcome of Sammy's trial. Mrs. Kaminsky appeared to be in denial about the whole catastrophe. Alicia was not ready to smell the symbolic roses I had offered up; Masters' mastery of courtroom manipulation and the weakness of the circumstantial evidence didn't impress her.

I was an actor playing to a non-responsive audience. Those of us who have emerged from the privileged classes live under the delusion that the future will always be fortuitous; we see that as our birthright. It may be impossible for us to understand, therefore, how the struggling masses view Lady Fate as the belligerent handmaiden of a malevolent deity; one who twists the threads of gracious possibility into a hopelessly tangled hangman's noose of a rope which, as one pulls and tugs upon it, only tightens and strangles.

Perspective differs according to one's vantage point. And I was now viewing Mrs. Kaminsky's modest meal as ambrosial, scrumptious, as toothsome as the most splendid spread of blue plate ever laid by Henrici's. I could ignore the miss-matched water glasses and the chipped china as I sank into a sea of tangy sauerkraut and delectably starchy potatoes which transported me to an Old World where the flavors and textures of ordinary edibles sang songs of hard-worked earth and fresh, breathable air.

I was half-way through the cheesecake when we heard a rattling at the rear entrance. It seemed to me that the Mister was coming through the back door, disoriented from strong drink and a world transformed by drifting snow. But it was not he. Alicia's exclamation as she opened the door stunned us all: "Sammy!"

In tumbled Sammy Kaminsky, striped prison clothes caked with ice, face reddened from the cold. He collapsed, panting, on the kitchen floor. Alicia began rubbing his bare hands. I ran to collect my heavy overcoat and brought it to drape around the frozen young man's shivering shoulders. I was very worried about frost bite and thought we should call for a doctor. When I suggested this, Alicia shook her head.

"They'd only throw him back in jail," she said. "Back into a cold cell where he'd die of pneumonia. Help me up with him."

Together we managed to bring Sammy into the parlor where there was a small fire smoldering in the fireplace. I threw some sticks of wood on it and stoked it up to a warming blaze. We pulled an arm chair in front of the fireplace and hefted Sammy onto it. He seemed dazed. His eyes were fluttering and his head bobbed. All at once he seemed to wake and sat upright with an anguished look on his face. He blurted out in Polish:

"Pomocy! Dokąd mnie zabieracie? Nie zrobiłem nic złego! Nie! Nie! Policja! Policja! Zostaw mnie!"

Then he fell back and his eyes closed. I asked Alicia what he had said.

"He said, 'Where are you taking me? I've done nothing wrong. Leave me alone.' And something about no police."

Mrs. Kaminsky was in tears. "Mój chłopak...mój biedny

chłopak!" she kept saying over and over. It didn't need translation—she was obviously distraught. I tried to comfort her while Alicia worked on reviving Sammy. I sent Stephen into the kitchen to fetch some hot coffee. After what seemed like hours but was probably only a matter of tens of minutes, Sammy's shivering ceased and he was able to sip some coffee. I...we...were desperate to find out why Sammy was here, how he got here. But we waited as he thawed, returning from a frozen state, nearly dead, and certainly exhausted. Finally he spoke, at first in broken sentences punctuated by strong inhalations and wheezes, like a cold motor struggling to turn over. Then he found his voice.

"I was told I was to be transferred from Hubbard Street to the South Side. There was some sort of mix up...I don't know what. They kept calling me 'Andrews.' A police van was waiting. I could take my belongings...these were wrapped in a dirty cloth...a few pictures and the watch Papa gave me on my sixteenth birthday. They had taken these things from me when first I arrived in that horrible place. I didn't understand what was happening...why they gave me the watch back...unless they were taking me not to another jail, but to a place to await execution! I hadn't had a trial yet, had I? How could they do that?

"I was pushed into the van. They didn't bother to chain me to the railing inside. I guess they thought I could not escape from that solid metal box with its single barred window. It was freezing inside and out. There was no blanket or other protection from the cold. I was a pig to the slaughter...at least that is what I thought. The van started up with a jerk that nearly knocked me over. I struggled to my feet to peer out of the window. I watched as we slowly made our way across the river on the Dearborn Street Bridge. There was a tug pushing a barge through broken ice flows below. I remember thinking how the billows of coal black smoke that rose from its stacks contrasted with the fiercely falling clumps of white snow...how neither could overpower or extinguish the other. Man versus nature...strange thoughts for a condemned man!

"We were at the south end of the Loop because I recognized some of the buildings. The police van was slipping a lot in the snow and of a sudden we became stuck in a drift. There were two cops in the front who began cursing in language that shocked even me. The wheels spun and the van settled ever more down into the snow and the mud. It was clearly not going anywhere. I would have laughed had I not been frightened out of my mind. Then a strange thing happened: the policemen left the van. I could see them from out of the window as they walked around the corner at Cullerton Avenue and entered what I knew to be a saloon, one of Dago Frank's, I think. We had reached the Levee and the cops were obviously going to wait out the storm with a little recreation! I was still stuck in a freezing cold police van. I tried to remember some of those prayers you taught me, Mama.

"I banged on the door with both of my fists, hoping the cops would hear and remember they had left me here in the cold. But they were gone. Perhaps one of the denizens of the district would take pity on me and arrive with a crow bar to extract me from this refrigerated prison on wheels. Jack Wynch's and Vic Shaw's were just down the block and many of their regulars hated the Chicago cops. But as I pounded harder and harder I could feel the door beginning to buckle. I threw all my weight into it…oh, I know, I'm skinny and not strong…but I was on fire inside. I attacked that door with a fury that surprised me. And it gave!

"I fell out onto the snow. I saw immediately that the Chicago City Railway car barns were just down the street. I made for them. At least I could hide in a place of relative warmth. None of the electric streetcars would be moving through this snow, I knew. Inside the barn were two or three abandoned horse-drawn trolleys, no longer used since electric wiring had been installed throughout the city. I found a discarded horse blanket and curled up in one of the trolleys. I hoped I'd be safe there at least until dark when I could make my way to…where? Where could I go that the authorities wouldn't search for me?

"If I could get to the underground tunnels I could connect with an interurban or a freight going out of state. But I had no money and I was still dressed in prison clothing. I tried to sleep…I couldn't. I lay there, wrapped in that evil smelling, moldy old blanket, still shivering. Then I heard a scraping sound and a thump up on the roof. And more thumping. Rats? Police closing in on me? I thought to run but I was so tired, so afraid…I could only wait and face my fate reluctantly, sadly. I wished above all things, as this dreadful noise grew louder and closer, that I could see you one more time, Mama, before…

"There was a broken window over where I huddled. Two eyes appeared, glowing in the semi-darkness like those of some demon from hell. But I had to laugh—it was only an alley cat, bedraggled and lonely and as cold as I was. Come here cat. I won't hurt you. But she scampered away. Two lonely, frightened beings in a merciless frozen world! I tried again to sleep. At least I now had a plan: to return home. They would catch me certainly, for they would search there...but I would have a few precious moments with my matka, my braciszek, my siostrzyca.

"It grew darker inside of the car barn, which meant evening had arrived outside. I moved cautiously from the trolley and peered out one of the barn's small windows. Yes! Dusk had fallen and now I could venture outside and try to make my way home without being seen. Can you imagine the fear and trepidation I felt? Anyone I encountered would instantly recognize my prison clothing and call for a policeman. But one no was abroad. The wind was too fierce and blowing snow made traveling near to impossible—impossible for me as well. If only there had still been horses in use...damn electricity!

"I threw the horse blanket over my shoulders for at least some protection from the wind and made my way out into the street. As I crept through the Levee I saw, incredibly, revelers moving from bar to bar...even in this blisteringly cold winter night! No one took notice of me. I was just another errant soul wandering through that wilderness of sin and debauchment. I saw that if I stayed close to buildings on the south side of the street I could avoid the deepest drifts and so I went, my prison-issue shoes wet, the cuffs of my pants filled with ice. It was like visiting the North Pole dressed in pajamas.

"I staggered along like this for four or five blocks until I came to the railroad tracks that ran along the east bank of the river. I stood on the banks of that ice clogged waterway considering whether to throw myself into its chilling depths. Then along came a tug boat pulling a barge. There was a bit of a bend to the river where I stood and the barge had to angle close to me to make the turn. On an impulse I jumped. I've never been much of an athlete but I could have won the broad jump with the effort I put into that leap of...what? Faith? Fate?

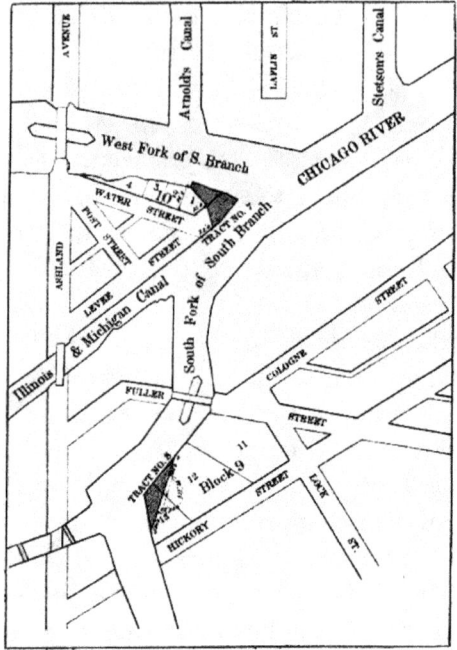

"It was empty, that rusting iron behemoth. I landed with a loud thud that I was sure would attract the crew of the tug, but apparently they heard nothing over the normal creaks and groans of the barge. I hid in the shadows. I thought perhaps they were headed to the Illinois Ship Canal that connected the Chicago River to the Des Plaines River. If I stayed on the barge…and didn't freeze to death, I could be out of the county in no time. But soon I saw that the barge was being shoved up against a pier…ungraciously I should say, with banging and bumping and the shriek of metal against wood. I ventured to look over the railing and discovered we had docked at one of the slips that ran out from the Union Stock Yards. Longshoremen were securing the barge with thick ropes. I cowered under my blanket.

"Did the stock yards run all day *and* all night? Would workers be dragging bloody carcasses out to dump into the barge on top of me? Would they fill it with entrails and bones to transport to the Bubbly Creek? The Creek! Of course! That foul drain was connected somehow to this part of the river. If I could find it, I could follow it—it would take me home. Cautiously I raised myself up and over the high side of the barge. No one was in evidence. I climbed onto the pier and tried to orient myself—which way was south? West? Home? I moved along the waterfront, keeping the river on my right reasoning that the flow was south and east. I soon came to a great fetid pool where no ice had formed and the water appeared reddish-brown and flecked with floating offal. I skirted this and began following a narrowing stream that surely was Bubbly Creek.

"The snow has drifted and I sink into it at times up to my waist. I am making little progress...pull my feet up and out of the drift, push forward, sink again. Beat my hands against my frozen thighs. Lean into the wind. Find higher ground where the snow isn't so deep...impossible! Can't feel my feet, my hands. My face is numb, my eyelids are freezing and I must blink constantly in order to see. The wind sends shards of ice crystals and frozen snow to buffet me and pound me into submission. I must go on. Or? Or I could lie down here under this soft white blanket and sleep.

"I saw a dull orange glow. Dots of light which became the squares of windows as I drew near. The sparkle of a dozen street lamps coming on along the deserted streets of Ducktown, all at once, as if to welcome me home. But the lights were on the opposite side of the creek. There are, of course, no bridges over that disgusting ditch at that point. I was so close...and yet so far away. That creek doesn't freeze. It isn't composed of enough actual water—only the liquefied sinews and guts of those dear animals we slaughter for the pleasure of our table. I couldn't leap across and I wasn't about to venture into its evil fluids. Ahead I spotted a small island. Perhaps I could manage to jump...

"One leg slipped into the muck at the edge of the island where I landed. I was repulsed but I could not stop to worry about that small unpleasantness. The island was a bit farther from the opposite bank which I now needed to gain, but I jumped...and landed sprawled against a cold, muddy incline. I was slipping steadily down toward the Bubbly Creek. My hands seemed unable to find purchase. I doubled my effort, grabbed and clawed and worked with my knees and my feet to push my way up that slippery slope. Found a root. Pulled. Made it out of the creek bed and lay panting in the snow, too tired to even shiver anymore.

"I still had about a mile to go before I would reach the house. I told myself if I gave up now, I didn't deserve to live. My choice was to find the strength to go on, to conquer the cold and the fatigue and the fear. I struggled to my feet, lumbered onward. No one was abroad in that desolate winterscape. No one to find my frozen body covered in snow if I failed.

"The last few yards before I reached the door of this house were the greatest ordeal of my life! I was Sisyphus, struggling under the weight of that enormous bolder I was to push forever up hill. I was Tantalus, eternally and hopelessly reaching for life-giving fruit dangling just beyond reach. I was Samuel Kaminsky, whose ice-shrouded legs had lost the strength to rise up out of the snow—I crawled the last few agonizing steps. Pulled myself up against the door, wrenched it open, and fell finally into the succor of the warmth of this household."

We remained silent, allowing Sammy to rest. We heaped blankets upon him, rubbed his legs and arms. I didn't see any evidence of severe frostbite, but I wanted him to be examined by a doctor. I told Alicia and her mother that I would transport Sammy to my own apartment tonight; he couldn't stay here where the police were sure to search. I was about to suggest we place him into a warm bath, when there was a loud banging at the front door. The police? Would all the torment he had endured now be in vain? Alicia and I lifted Sammy and between us managed to drag him into the pantry: not a sufficient hiding place, but perhaps if I could convince the police not to search the house...

I went to door, opened it. I was relieved to see that it was only my sled driver, just arrived to collect me. This small scare now motivated me to hurry home with Sammy bundled up against the cold, next to me in sled. I was going to be guilty of aiding and abetting a fugitive!

12

The Confession

Fresh snow is imbued with a kind of magic; it transforms, encases the ugliness of the city with an otherworldly majesty. But a day or two of industry as usual, and soot and grime paint over the crystal fantasy with a patina of corruption, a deformity of environment that shocks rather than delights. The softness compacts. Shovels gouge great caverns through the byways, heap up hills of flake and slush to further perturb the eye.

The penetrating cold lingers. Fires burn gladly in my rooms—I have a fireplace on each floor, stoked religiously by George Mandel. George and his wife have shown no curiosity about my house guest; Minnie, my maid, however, is bursting to ask who it is who occupies the upper floor and takes his meals alone. Who never ventures past the front door. Who never stands near windows unless the curtains are drawn. Sammy, the small, frightened man-boy. Sammy, the fugitive from justice! Sammy, the unjustly accused? And here was I, in the curious position of trying to protect three different people…all of whom might very well be guilty!

When I arrived at the club I found Rodney in his usual pose: slumped in his easy chair, half slumbering, one hand on a beaker of brandy, the other clutching a smoldering cigar. He acknowledged me with this:

"What ever you do, old fellow, don't mention your house guest to Masters. He can't be a party to…"

"How did you…what do you know?" I queried.

"I read the newspapers. It is a simple thing to deduce the location of our friend."

I glanced around the room. The other members were seated far enough from us that I wasn't concerned they might overhear. But I kept my voice low. "What am I to do? If I can't contact Masters, and I can't convince Sammy to give himself up, there doesn't seem to be a solution."

"There is the obvious solution. I'm surprised you haven't thought of it yet."

Now came one of those long pauses in which it seemed time stood still; the hands on the clock refused to advance; the sun would never set; my breathing had stopped. Rodney was, of course, waiting for me to utter, "What?"

"You must obtain a confession from the one who never came forward."

"Connie."

"Yes, Connie."

Again I stood on the front stairs of the Dunning mansion, waiting for the butler to answer my knock. The statue of Pan leered at me from one side of that elaborate portal and a brazen Aphrodite smiled seductively from the other. The gods were watching me, judging me. And I was judging myself! I didn't think Sammy had killed Willard Dunning, at least not by himself. However, his escape, should he be apprehended, would surely seal his doom—I could not allow that to happen. And now my task to somehow wrench a confession from Connie had placed me between Scylla and Charybdis. I couldn't save one without condemning the other.

The door opened and I was ushered into the parlor. The potted ferns had dried out and their once delicate fronds had curled into brown clumps; some had fallen to the dusty floor. The heavy drapes were drawn across the windows. An ominous gloom pervaded the interior of the Dunning mansion that morning. A maid appeared to ask if I wanted coffee or tea. I waved her away.

Connie entered, dressed in a floor-length frock that seemed overly formal for everyday attire. Yet I could see that the dress was wrinkled and stained in one or two places, as if she had not changed her clothing recently. Her hair, usually piled high and secured with sparkling hairpins was coming loose; strands rolled onto her forehead and down the back of her neck, swaying as she swung into the room. In the past, when she moved...so light and carefree, I would have said she floated—now she seemed composed of an unwieldy density, as if she carried with her the weight of the world.

We sat together on the velvet davenport, silent except for the trivial how-are-you and good-to-see-you. She knew why I had come. Prolonging the moment was useless. I spoke to the matter, without passion or contempt. I affirmed my absolute regard for her well-being. I appealed to her conscience, hinted at the ravages of long held guilt. I rattled on with as much authority as I could muster about the propensity of the justice system for siding with the fair sex. And all this without an accusation. Nor would I ask that fatal question: did she, or didn't she? And why?

Hate and fear are inexorably linked in the human condition. Those extrinsic forces that combine to forge one's very being are the cement that binds them and binds us to them. We are predisposed toward both fight and flight when goaded. Which turning we take is the stuff of happenstance...or is it? That she might have planned to eliminate the pain she felt through calculated action was a possibility I preferred to discount. It was the passion of the moment that clutched that statue of The Thinker, brought metal down against flesh, spilled the life-force of the offending obstacle...the brutal parent. I didn't...couldn't ask.

Connie: "Yes, I killed him. Given the circumstances, it's not incredible that I acted as I did. I am not looking for sympathy or understanding. I cannot justify the murder by anything but the inevitability that survival depends upon vanquishing evil. You don't know...you can't understand how it was...what he was."

I answered: "I do understand, Connie. Your father's treatment of Peter and Sammy...his rejection of their lifestyle..."

"Peter and Sammy? No. I didn't much care for their 'lifestyle,' as you call it. It was unnatural. It flew in the face of all that is holy. I pitied Peter, but I didn't kill for him."

"Then I don't understand...unless..."

"If Peter was an aberration it was in his blood. The sins of the father are often visited upon the offspring. Father's perversion was unthinkable, inhuman, demonic. Yes, he was the devil incarnate! I believe that."

"He abused you."

"Both of us. I can't talk about it. But it went on for years and years. It started with little games he would play with us. Then…"

"Don't you see, Connie, that this is a defense? I don't mean to be cold-blooded, but a jury would never convict you knowing the truth."

"Don't you see that I can never come out in the open? I can't tell. It would kill my mother. All the people that know us. I can't do it."

"Just tell me this then: did you plan it, or was it an impulse of the moment?"

"Peter and I often talked about killing father. We dreamed up wonderful scenarios in which he suffered terribly. Push him off a tall building; throw him under the wheels of a horse cart; set him on fire! Personally, I liked the idea of drowning him…holding him under and watching him struggle. But no, we were only children fantasizing. I didn't know I was going to strike him that day. I barely remember doing it. We were arguing about Peter and Sammy. He made me so mad…I just…"

"All right, I believe you. But we can't let Sammy be prosecuted for this. Please let me take you to talk with Edgar Masters, the attorney. Or maybe I could get Darrow."

"No…Masters. I don't like Darrow."

"You'll come?"

"I'll talk to him. But I'll never…"

A crash—fragments of a porcelain vase scattering, rivulets of stale water splashing, dried hard nodules of dead flowers striking the dusty floor—but no scream, no gasp, no thrown-up hands from the still figure standing in the doorway. Only an open mouth, astonished eyes. How long had Connie's mother been there, listening?

"Mother!"

"Mrs. Dunning, let me…"

"Oh…no…Connie. That can't be true. It just can't be true!"

"My grandfather knew Lincoln very well. And my father once practiced law with William Herndon, Lincoln's law partner in the early days. In spite of the laurels heaped upon our 16th president by people like Sandburg, Lincoln was a fraud and an enemy of the people!"

"But Mr. Masters," I said after hearing this tirade against one of my heros, " 'Honest Abe' freed the slaves and brought the Union back together."

"Sir! Lincoln was devious—smart like a fox, I'll warrant—but blundering and self-interested to the extent of bringing on the Civil War for his own purposes, shifting power to the Federal Government, ignoring civil liberties, courting financial interests…and, he was a sexual deviate!"

"Well, that's a little harsh. I'm sorry I brought up the idea of Lincoln as a saint, Mr. Masters. I was really here to ask you to talk to Constance Dunning. You know that Samuel Kaminsky was arrested for the murder of her father, and that he escaped. Connie…Miss Dunning has something to say in the matter that I think you should hear."

"Very well," said Masters, lining up some of pencils and pens that had lain in disarray on the blotter on his desk and forming a pattern that looked like a miniature pyramid. (Was he a Freemason?) "Silence can poison the soul," he continued. "Loosening the tongue, while often unruly and certainly terrifying under certain circumstances like this, can nonetheless forestall misfortune. Bring the young lady into my chambers and let her speak to me in private, if you will."

I summoned Connie from the waiting room and did as Masters requested, leaving her with the old curmudgeon. I hadn't meant to get into a political argument with him and I was sorry I had, for surely his recent temper would cause him to be less than tolerant with Connie. What transpired, and what either said to the other I would not be privy to, but the aftermath was satisfying indeed. Connie emerged, not exactly smiling, but obviously relieved and apparently fortified by her tête-à-tête with the attorney. We would be going to the authorities, she would confess and explain her hesitation in coming forward, she would help to exonerate Sammy of complicity in the crime, and she would go to trial, represented by the brilliant Edgar Lee Masters, and be acquitted once and for all!

Maclay Hoyne, the Cook County State's Attorney who had so famously and successfully battled corruption and conspiracy in the Chicago Police Department, who had a stellar conviction record, who had released a public statement on the subject of women accused of murder, to whit: "this office does not recognize the 'unwritten law' and it will behoove defense attorneys to actually present facts to the court," Maclay Hoyne, who Edgar Lee Maasters characterized as "a scourge-wielder, balance-wrecker, smiter with whips and swords (of the law), hater of breakers of the law, legalist, inexorable and bitter," *this* Maclay Hoyne took personal charge of the case of the County of Cook verses Miss Constance Dunning.

At first Hoyne refused to even listen to Connie's confession. It was, he said, a Mongolian cluster-fuck. They'd had four different confessions, a mistrial over a falsely accused man, an escaped defendant, and more bad publicity than the allegedly corrupt and mismanaged legal system could endure. Masters, however, had friends in the Chicago Police Department's Division of Investigation. Through these contacts, he had discovered that in an evidence locker at the Hubbard Street station, someone had bagged, labeled and stored the small statue which had been found to be the murder weapon.

Masters contacted Edward Foster, the man who had testified in the landmark Chicago trial of Thomas Jennings, the first American convicted of murder through the evidence of fingerprints. Foster was a fingerprint expert and agreed to examine the statue. Masters immediately told reporters from all the Chicago newspapers that new evidence could be presented in the Dunning murder case, if only State's Attorney Hoyne would agree to release the murder weapon to his investigator. The Kaminsky boy was innocent, Masters told the papers, and fingerprints would prove it. The newspapers ran with the idea and pressure of public opinion finally convinced Hoyne to reopen the case.

Foster was able to lift a finger and thumb print from the stature. These, although somewhat smeared, matched a fresh set taken from Connie Dunning. There were legal considerations to dropping the case against Sammy and subsequently charging Connie, but Hoyne seemed able to maneuver sufficiently, with the help of Judge Herman James Hoffmeyer, (the judge who had officiated at the first trial in which Willy Borman had almost been railroaded to the gallows). Writs and motions and procedures and back-room meetings took place; apparently everyone concerned was eager to finally put the case to rest. Connie was charged, arraigned and went to trial on February 3, the day the 16th Amendment to the United States Constitution was ratified, authorizing the Federal government to impose and collect income taxes.

Of the initial proceedings of that trial there would be nothing to tell that wasn't mundane, stuffy, even boring. It did seem to me to go on forever with countless repeated testimony from police and crime lab officials who painstakingly established the authenticity of the murder weapon and its damning fingerprints. Edward Foster testified for the prosecution, illustrating his conclusions with large poster-sized blow-ups of the fingerprints; juries were still not used to fingerprint evidence and may have been skeptical of the science behind it. Masters had no questions.

Masters wisely would not let Connie testify. His only witness was her brother, Peter. Through carefully crafted questions he tried to establish the threat Connie's father posed for her. He had been admonished to refrain from asking about sexual abuse, but cleverly left the jury wondering if in fact there was such a history.

"Did your father ever strike your sister?"

"Yes."

"On more than one occasion?"

"Yes, many times."

"Can you offer any explanation for his unusually brutal treatment of her?"

"Objection, your Honor!" (This from the prosecuting attorney.)

"Sustained. The counselor will refrain from leading the witness." (This from the judge.)

"In your opinion, was the amount of physical punishment heaped upon your sister appropriate to some misbehavior on her part? We all know the old adage, 'spare the rod and spoil the child.' Was it appropriate or not?"

"My sister was always obedient and respectful both to our father and mother. She never misbehaved."

"Why then, do you suppose he hit her?"

"I...I can't say."

"Did he ever touch her in any other way? I'm sorry, your Honor. I withdraw the question."

Would it be enough, I wondered? How many of the jury "spared the rod" with their own children? Not many, I supposed. That a fine upstanding citizen like Willard Dunning might sexually abuse his own daughter—well, that was unthinkable. Without Peter's abuse brought into the light, thereby offering an eye-witness account, it would have been impossible to prove. Yet, Masters had a tactic. His closing would be persuasive...I hoped.

The prosecutor, in his closing argument, instructed jurors "not to consider the 'unwritten law' and to rely only upon the facts." The fact was, he told the gentlemen of the jury, that Constance Dunning had willfully and deliberately murdered her father and deserved the full penalty of the law for the despicable act of patricide.

Edgar Lee Masters, in a passionate plea to the jury, argued that Connie had only been defending herself. There was such a thing, he told them, as "self-defense in advance." There was a "*new* unwritten law" which gave a woman the right to kill any man who betrayed or abused her, even if she used the violence in a pre-emptive way. I scanned the faces of the jurors, trying to discern whether sympathy or empathy had been established, but they wore faces of stone.

What did I, myself, think bout this new unwritten law? I had to admit that self-defense was and should be excusable. But self-defense in advance? So now we waited while the jury deliberated. Even Masters himself was unsure of the verdict. It was hours later when I talked to him in the hallway of the courthouse. The jury was still out.

"We could hope for a hung jury," he said. "That might be the best we could hope for."

"They're taking their sweet time about it. There must be some doubt in at least some of their minds," I said.

"I just wish I could have used the sexual abuse argument. There would be no question that the new unwritten law would apply. But I guess some things are to be feared more than the gallows. Propriety, shame, guilt...victims often blame themselves for the misconduct of others."

"You did all you could do."

"The rest is up to fate...and a jury of her peers. Twelve men who ought to have to wrestle with their consciences, but who will be led by the strongest, or the loudest, among them. Twelve typical Americans. Schooled too little or too much. Learning only about safety first. Joining the church and abandoning the quest for truth. Doing their duty out of superstition and ignorance. Anxious to be home for supper in good time."

"So why are they taking so long?"

"One hold-out I suspect. One good and true man who will crumble under pressure at the end and vote with the rest."

And at that cheery thought the bailiff called the officers of the court back: the jury had returned.

"Gentlemen of the jury, have you reached a verdict?" asked the judge after the jury had filed in.

The foreman stood. "Yes, your Honor, we have."

"How find you?"

"In the case of the State against Constance Dunning, in the matter of the death of Willard Dunning, we the jury find the defendant guilty of murder in the first degree."

Byron Grush

Epilogue

I married the girl, of course. Alicia and I brought her mother, the baby and the youngest son, Stephen, to live with us at the house on North Astor Street. Getting them away from that horrible Ducktown was one of the few things I am proud of in this life. Peter and Sammy moved to New York City where they could live their lives in a more accepting environment—the notoriety of the trial gave them little chance of anonymity in Chicago.

Connie's appeal ended in a mistrial. She will probably be incarcerated indefinitely unless some legal legerdemain can accomplish her release. Edgar Lee Masters has washed his hands of the matter, and of lawyering in general. He has been devoting his time to writing and a series of poems he published in the Reedy's Mirror as Webster Ford have just been reissued under his own name as *Spoon River Anthology*. I was delighted to read that this has been well received; the man has a sort of genius, and definitely a point of view.

My greatest concern these days is for the future of our country. There is a great war raging in Europe and thus far, Wilson has kept us out of it. But just this last May the liner Lusitania was torpedoed and sunk by a German submarine. Sinking an unarmed passenger vessel is being seen as a heinous act by the Germans and will surely add fuel to the fire for those who would plunge us into the conflict. Rodney recently told me (how he was privy to classified information has always been a puzzlement to me) that the Lusitania was carrying war munitions such as artillery shells and the gun cotton and the aluminum powder used to manufacture explosives. If we do enter the war, my chief concern will be for Stephen. He is now 16 and he will want to fight.

You are probably wondering if I ever learned the solution to that other mystery, the one about the murder in the locked room. Rodney never told me. The whole game of puzzles which we played was eclipsed by that real world murder and the subsequent trials. We never returned to our quizzical pastime, having had quite enough trauma and intrigue to last us for a very long time. Perhaps you have figured out who killed who and how. Or perhaps not.

About the Author

Byron Grush was born and raised in Naperville, Illinois, just southwest of Chicago. He is a third generation native of that town. Grush studied art and design at the University of Illinois and filmmaking at the School of the Art Institute of Chicago. At the Art Institute he was a student of Gregory Markopoulos, one of the originators of the New America Cinema movement in the 1960s.

Grush then taught at The School of the Art Institute of Chicago, creating a course in film animation in the mid-seventies. He later became an Associate Professor at the College of Art at Northern Illinois University in Dekalb, Illinois, where he taught in the Electronic Media area. He is the author of a book on hand-drawn animation techniques entitled *The Shoestring Animator*. Becoming interested in genealogy, he wrote a trilogy of historical novels based upon what he had learned about his early ancestors.

He and his wife moved to New Mexico in the late 1990s, and opened an art gallery featuring Outsider and Visionary Art in Santa Fe. They returned to the Midwest to retire in the small town of Delavan, Wisconsin, a place that reminds them of their roots. Grush writes, paints and studies Tai Chi.

Other fiction by Byron Grush

All The Way By Water
In which Isaac Grosh brings his wife and eight children to Illinois, traveling by flatboat on the Ohio and Mississippi Rivers.

Once Upon a Gold Rush
In which John and James Grosh journey by wagon train to California during the gold rush of '49. Introduces the characters of White Cloud and Little Wind.

Road of Stars
In which White Cloud searches for his father (James Grosh) and helps to build the Transcontinental Railroad.

Dance Beneath A Diamond Sky
This historical novel of the Sixties follows a group of young people as they search for identity, love, honor and redemption during the decade or so between the assassination of President John F. Kennedy and the resignation of Richard Nixon.

Violet at The Breakers: a novella
Violet might only have been twelve, but she was worldly. When her mother brought her and her sisters to Palm Beach, she hadn't expected to discover the body of a murdered man, or to be pursued by his killer. Nor had she expected a certain lady would be careless with a curling iron...

Romeo's Revenge and Other Wisconsin Stories
An anthology of twelve short stories about the towns and people of Wisconsin.

www.ingramcontent.com/pod-product-compliance
Lightning Source LLC
Chambersburg PA
CBHW060631130626
46555CB00002B/746